HAL

D1602860

HAL

Mary Blakeslee

A GEMINI BOOK

Published in 1995 by
Stoddart Publishing Co. Limited
34 Lesmill Road
Toronto, Canada
M3B 2T6
(416) 445-3333

First published in 1991 as an Irwin Young Adult Book by
Stoddart Publishing Co. Limited

Canadian Cataloguing in Publication Data

Blakeslee, Mary
Hal

"A Gemini book."
ISBN 0-7736-7432-2

I. Title.

PS8553.L35H3 1994   jC813'.54   C94-932830-8
PZ7.B53Ha 1994

Cover Design: Brant Cowie/ArtPlus Limited
Cover Illustration: Albert Slark
Typesetting: Tony Gordon Ltd.

Printed and bound in Canada

*Stoddart Publishing gratefully acknowledges the support of
the Canada Council, Ontario Ministry of Culture, Tourism,
and Recreation, Ontario Arts Council, and Ontario
Publishing Centre in the development of writing
and publishing in Canada.*

One

"It'll be all right, Hal. Pete will take you over to the high school while classes are out for Christmas vacation and help you familiarize yourself with the layout."

Mom patted my hand, then gently put my fingers around the handle of the cup of cocoa she had placed in front of me. "Careful, it's hot," she warned. I heard her move away and pull out a chair across the kitchen table from me.

Dad's voice came from my right. "Of course you'll do just fine, son," he said, his voice unnaturally cheerful. "You and Pete will be in all the same classes, so he'll always be there to help you."

I slammed down the cup and felt the hot cocoa slop onto my wrist. "How do you know Pete will be in the same classes?" I demanded. "The high school has over three hundred Grade 11 students, so the chance of us being in all the same classes is very remote. Unless, of course, you arranged it that way!"

I could almost taste the tension in the air as my mother, father and brother held their collective breath. I could also read their minds: there he goes again, blowing up over nothing. But we must be patient. It's so very hard for him.

It had been like this for the past two weeks, ever since I had come home to stay. I'd been living at the school for the blind back east for the past ten years, ever since I lost my sight when I was seven years old. I had made regular trips home for Christmas and Easter and for a week or two in the summer, but that wasn't the same as living at home permanently — and going to a regular high school.

"He isn't cooperating, Mrs. Drucker," the principal had written my mom. "He has been a disrupting influence on the rest of the student body and a trial to the teachers for some time. However, we were unwilling to take drastic measures until he went beyond all bounds of gentlemanly conduct. So I am compelled to inform you that he will no longer be welcome at our school." I guess I'm the only guy in history who's been expelled from a school for the blind! I can still remember the day it happened.

We were filing out of the dining hall from breakfast, in line as usual, when Louie "The Goon" Lyle, the phys ed instructor and dining room monitor, grabbed poor old Richie Harris and pulled him aside. I was walking just behind Richie, so I was right there when The Goon started giving Richie a bad time.

Hey, would you look at that?" he said to the world in general. "The kid's got his pants on inside out." Then he started to laugh this high maniacal whinny that accompanied all his sadistic little plays.

"I wondered what those flaps were," Richie answered, all innocent. "I guess it's my pockets."

That caused The Goon to laugh even harder. Then while the whole line stood waiting and listening he suddenly turned nasty. "Okay, Harris. You've got five minutes to get back to the dorm and dress yourself properly. Then I'll expect to see you out on the field for fifty laps before your next class."

Richie began to whimper and I heard him half stumble. The Goon must have pushed him. Richie was hardly able to stay in an upright position at the best of times since he was not only blind and mentally disabled but also spastic, and punishing him with fifty laps was totally sadistic. At that moment I saw red — literally. My whole brain exploded and the next thing I knew I was standing over The Goon who was lying on the floor screaming at me.

"You hit me, you little piece of scum!" he roared. "How dare you!"

I heard him start to get up and then he was grabbing my shirt. I pushed his hand away and was ready to paste him again when my arm was caught from behind.

"All right — enough, Drucker." Harry Handy, the other dining room monitor, spoke out. "Lyle, get this line moving. Drucker, you come with me."

I spent the next hour in the principal's office being lectured on the evils of physical agression, respecting your elders and other quaint myths. Then I was given the opportunity of either apologizing to The Goon or leaving the school for good. I picked the latter.

So here I was back home to stay and scared out of my gourd. But there was no way I was going to let anyone know how I felt. And I sure as hell wasn't going to spend the rest of the year being baby-sat by my younger brother.

"*Did* you arrange it?" I demanded.

"Well, sort of," Dad hedged. "We all thought it would be best for you to have someone to . . ."

"Well, you can just un-arrange it. I won't be treated like a three-year-old." I stood up and started to walk away from the table. Suddenly I felt a pull on my right arm, and the next thing I knew the dishes and cutlery were crashing onto the floor behind me. I grabbed at my sleeve and discovered my identification bracelet had caught on the table-cloth.

There was dead silence, then Mom, determinedly calm, murmured, "It's okay, dear. No harm done."

Sure. No harm done to the dishes, maybe. But what about me? I knew I was acting like a jerk and making everyone uncomfortable, but I couldn't seem to stop myself from lashing out whenever I was treated as *different*. In less than a week I'd be facing my first day as a regular student at Churchill High, and the closer the time came, the less sure I was that I'd be able to cope. Fear, my counselor at the school used to tell me, can turn the gentlest person into an ogre. Boy, did he ever get *that* right!

I muttered an apology and bent to help pick up the mess. I was groping around for stray pieces of crockery when Mom put a restraining hand on my arm.

"Never mind, dear, I've got it under control," she assured me. "Run along and finish dressing. Dad will drive you and Pete over to the school on his way to work."

What else could I do? I got up and went to my room.

* * *

"Need any help?" Pete's voice came from the doorway as I was slipping my blue sweater over my head.

"No thanks," I answered. "I'm just about ready."

Pete came farther into the room. "You look good, Hal — all coordinated. How do you manage to get the right stuff together?"

"Braille labels," I answered and showed him where I'd had little plastic strips sewn into my sweater and pants indicating their color. "Also I've got everything pretty well organized." I drew a comb through my hair and turned to him. "Okay, let's split. The sooner we get this over with, the better."

"Look, Hal, I'm really sorry about Dad getting

the principal to put us into the same classes. I told him you wouldn't like it, but he wouldn't listen. You know how he is. But don't worry; I'll fix it before school opens. I can sure see how you wouldn't want your little brother hanging around all the time. Might cramp your style." He laughed and took my arm.

I had a terrible urge to pull away but managed to control it. Pete was only trying to be helpful. As we walked together down the stairs and out to the car I thought about how it must be for him having his blind older brother suddenly appear in his life. We're only sixteen months apart, and since I missed a lot of school the year I lost my sight we're both in the same grade. If anyone's style was going to be cramped, I figured it would be Pete's, not mine. Somehow I was going to have to do everything I could to avoid being a drag, but it wouldn't be easy.

* * *

"I'll walk you to your homeroom if you like," Pete offered as we climbed the school steps five days later. "The first day after a holiday is always zoo time, what with all the kids milling around in the halls."

"That's okay," I answered. "I think I've got the layout pretty well memorized." I stopped and put my hand on his shoulder. "Thanks for everything. See you at three-thirty." As I moved carefully down the corridor toward the room Pete had pointed out as Mr. McGregor's, my homeroom and first period history teacher, I folded up my white cane and slipped it into my book bag. Stupid, I suppose, since the cane helps me avoid falling down stairs and crashing into walls. But it also identifies me as a blindie, and for some weird reason I wanted to start out looking like an ordinary guy.

True to his word, Pete had arranged that we wouldn't be in any classes together. He'd also done his best in orienting me to the maze of hallways and rooms that were Churchill High School. It sure was a different scene from the school for the blind I was used to. Three floors instead of one, no braille signs on the doors and about ten times as many students. Suddenly, as I turned the corner hoping I was in the right hallway, I wished with all my heart I was back there.

"Hey, watch where you're going, droog!" I jumped back and hit the wall behind me, dropping my book bag on my foot. The person I'd bumped into was still muttering to himself. "If you took those stupid shades off, you might avoid mowing down half the school."

"I'm sorry," I murmured, then bent to feel along the floor for my book bag. It wasn't where it had fallen, and I began groping around between legs trying to find it. I could feel the panic start as I moved down the hall still unable to locate it.

"Here, is this what you're looking for?" A soft female voice spoke above me. I stood up and turned toward it. An arm reached out and put the bag in my hand.

"Thanks," I muttered and started down the hall to where I hoped to find Mr. McGregor's room.

"My name is Nancy Adams," the voice said beside me, and I realized the girl was walking along with me. "You're new here, aren't you?"

"Yeah." My right hand was feeling along the wall, counting the open doorways. My homeroom was the third door along, *if* I was in the proper corridor. The book bag incident had disoriented me pretty badly.

"What's your name?"

"Ah, Hal — Hal Drucker." I wished she would leave so I could feel my way along to my classroom without the benefit of her curiosity.

"So what room are you looking for, Hal Drucker?" There was amusement in her voice, and I could feel myself bristle.

"Two thirty-four," I answered sharply. I had come to the third door on the right and was starting to turn in when I felt her hand on my arm.

"This is two ten," she said. "Two thirty-four is in the next corridor. Come on, I'll show you."

"That's okay. I can find it myself."

"Maybe so, but unless you start using your white cane you'll probably plow down half the student body before you get there."

I stopped and turned toward her voice. "It's that obvious, eh?"

"Not really, but I saw you stash your cane when you came in. Besides, I'm pretty used to blind people. My grandfather's been blind all my life."

Instead of steering me along like most people try to do, she put my hand on her arm and guided me back down the hall and into the proper corridor. A moment later we arrived at the open door to Mr. McGregor's room.

"Where's your last morning class?" she asked.

"The science lab," I told her. "Why?"

"I'll come and pick you up and take you to the caf if you like. It's kind of frantic around here at noon hour," she explained.

Oh, great! I just get rid of one baby-sitter and I land another! On the other hand, I realized I could use all the help I could get if I was going to ever find my way around this zoo. Getting from one place to another when the school was empty was a far cry from making it with a thousand kids milling around. I began to wish I hadn't been so hasty in having Pete get us into different classes, after all.

"Okay. Thanks." I tried to smile but it didn't come off very well, I guess.

"Don't worry," she said. "You'll be fine. Mr. McGregor is a neat teacher and the kids are mostly pretty okay." She pressed my hand and I heard her walk away.

More than anything in the world I wanted to bolt down the hall till I found an outside door and leave the school for good. But I didn't. I had to have an education and a good one if I was going to make it in the big, bad world. If I quit now, I could expect to spend the rest of my life making brooms. And nothing, not being embarrassed or hurt or scared to death, could be as bad as that.

I turned and felt my way into the classroom and to an empty seat at the front of the second row.

Two

I could tell the room was nearly empty. I took out my tape recorder and put my book bag on the floor. I read and write Grade 3 braille, which is about as high as you can go, but it's slow and awkward, so I use a tape recorder both to make notes to myself and to record class lectures. As I was checking the volume the bell rang and a gang of kids poured into the room. There was a lot of yelling back and forth as everyone seemed to talk at once, then one of those unnatural silences happened and the voice I had heard in the hall a few minutes before rang out.

"Hey, there's that creep in the sunglasses that nearly knocked me down. What's he doin' here?"

"Must be a transfer," a male voice answered.

The first voice, closer now, growled, "Well, he'd better keep outta my way if he knows what's good for him."

A laugh, then a girl's voice said, "Come off it,

Gord. Do you always have to go around proving how macho you are?"

The door slammed and someone in heavy shoes passed my desk and went up to the front of the room.

"Okay, enough already. Take your seats and settle down."

Mr. McGregor. He did sound neat, just like Nancy said. There was a rustling of paper and he began to call out:

"Adams, Kris?"

"Here."

"Arnold, Pamela?"

"Present, sir."

"Bidecker, Jacob?"

"Yo."

He continued through the attendance list until he hit my name.

"Drucker, Halford? Ah, yes. The newest member of our happy family. Welcome to the monkey house, Drucker. Hope you have a happy stay. Don't hesitate to call out if you require any assistance. Hadley, Gordon?"

The voice I was beginning to hate spoke out from the back in an exaggerated falsetto. "Here, Mr. McGregor, sir."

A couple of kids laughed, but the teacher ignored them and went on through the rest of the list. When he was through he went to the chalkboard and began to write. After a moment he put down the chalk and returned to his seat. That's your assignment for tomorrow. Now let's get down to business. Before the holidays we were talking about the reasons why Chamberlain signed the Munich Agreement with Hitler, Daladier and Mussolini in 1938."

I started my tape recorder and sat back to listen.

"Hey, no fair!" The offended voice of Gordon Hadley wailed from the back of the room. "How come the guy with the shades gets to use a tape recorder? You told us they were out of bounds in your class."

"Mr. Hadley," McGregor replied in an exasperated tone, "when and if you should ever lose your vision, as Mr. Drucker unfortunately has, you will have my full permission to use a tape recorder, too. Meanwhile, I would appreciate it if you would spend a little less time worrying about your classmates and a little more on the lesson I'm trying to teach."

There was an audible gasp from the class and a low murmur of voices filled the room. Then, the girl I'd heard call Hadley macho cried, "Honestly, Gord, sometimes you can be such a jerk!" Her voice was low and sultry, and even in anger she sounded totally sexy.

I felt my face get hot and I prayed I wasn't blushing. I bent my head and slid farther down in my seat. The worst things I had imagined were happening. The kids were embarrassed and uncomfortable about my blindness, and what was worse they were probably pitying me. So much for being just one of the guys. On top of all that, I'd made a major enemy of Gordon Hadley. He'd probably never let me forget that I'd made him look like a fool in front of his friends.

Mr. McGregor droned on about the invasion of Czechoslovakia but I wasn't paying any attention. Instead, I was trying to psych myself up for facing the class when the period was over and we were all filing out of the room.

As it turned out, I didn't need to worry. When the bell went, Mr. McGregor said, "If you'll stay for a moment, Drucker, I'll read the assignment into your tape recorder for you." By the time he was finished, the kids had all moved on to their next class and I was left in the corridor trying to remember where Pete had told me Mrs. Oliver's English lit class was being held.

I got through the rest of the morning with no other major calamities, probably because I got out my white cane and used it. Not only was I able to get down the halls without wiping anybody out, but it saved me the embarrassment I had felt in Mr. McGregor's class when he had to tell the kids I was blind.

True to her word, Nancy was waiting for me outside the science lab at eleven forty-five.

"How did it go, Hal?" she asked as she reached out her arm for me to take.

"Not so bad," I answered noncommittally. Then as she steered me through the crowd to the cafeteria I asked, "Who's that guy Gord Hadley? Do you know him?"

"Everybody knows Gross Gord," she answered. "He's Churchill High's resident loudmouth. He thinks he's hot spit because he shines on the football field, but basically he's a pain in the big toe." She paused, then in a quiet voice asked, "Why? Did you have another run-in with him?"

I told her about the incident in McGregor's class and how I figured I'd made an enemy for life.

"You're probably right, but don't let it throw you. Nobody takes Gord too seriously."

We had reached the cafeteria doors and Nancy stopped talking. I guess it took all her concentration to get through the crowd to the lineup at the counter. She was really great about getting my food for me without making a big production of it, and in less than ten minutes we were sitting together at a large table at the back of the room. There were already a number of people at the table talking. All the confidence I'd built up over the morning disappeared as I sat down with my tray of food.

Eating is not something a blind guy does with a lot of class. For one thing, it's hard to find the food on the plate and get it onto the fork. You can spend days trying to round up and impale a half a cup of peas, for instance. Then there's the problem of pouring liquid into a cup or glass. The only way it can be done without drowning yourself is to put your finger just over the rim so you can feel when the drink has reached the top. Not the most appetizing sight, I'm sure.

I sat there not moving for what seemed half the day, listening to the voices around me and wondering what to do about the food on my tray. Then a voice beside me spoke.

"Hi, my name is Horace Como, but my friends call me Hose. You're in my homeroom. Isn't Hadley a sleaze? Here, let me take the stuff off your tray. Do you play chess, by any chance? Ham at twelve o'clock, potatoes at eight and carrots at three. I've poured your milk and it's at the top left of your plate. Are you Pete Drucker's brother?" All this in a machine-gun delivery with a nonchalance that made me feel at ease for the first time that day. The guy even knew how to describe where the food was on the plate.

Nancy, who was sitting opposite me, spoke up.

"Hey, slow down, Hose. Give the guy a chance to eat before you demand his life history."

I laughed, (another first), and said, "That's okay. Yeah, I'm Pete's brother, and sure, I play chess."

"Great! The chess club meets after school on Tuesdays; that's today. I'll meet you in front of the office and take you to the club room. Did you know that chess originated in India around 500 AD? At least, that's what they think. Do you want any dessert? The apple crisp is almost edible."

It was impossible to keep up with the guy, so I just nodded. He could take that as either I knew about Indian chess or I'd like dessert. It didn't matter. But the chess club was a whole different story. I'd been playing chess since I was seven years old and just starting at the school for the blind. When I came home for vacation that summer Dad taught me how to play, hoping to help me develop my memory. It turned out I've got a very logical mind and took to the game like a duck to water, as they say, and it certainly did help me with memorizing. I can keep track of every piece without any trouble at all. Joining the chess club might be just the thing to show the kids I wasn't stupid just because I was blind.

When Hose came back with my apple crisp, I grinned and told him I'd really like to join the chess club and I'd be waiting for him after school. Then I remembered; Pete had his trumpet lesson on Tuesdays and wouldn't be able to wait around the school until the club was out to walk me home. It was only four blocks, but I had to cross a really busy street and I just wasn't ready to handle that on my own yet.

Hose must have figured something was wrong by the expression on my face and asked, "Any problems?"

I just couldn't tell him I couldn't get home after the meeting. It would have sounded so wimpy. "No problem, but I won't be able to make it today. Maybe next week."

"Gee, I'm sorry." And he really did sound disappointed. Not as disappointed as me, though. For the ten-thousandth time since those firecrackers went off in my face ten years ago and left me without my sight, I cursed the luck that had made me so damned helpless and dependent.

"What's your first period, Hal?" Nancy called across to me when the warning bell for afternoon classes rang.

"Math," I replied. "It's in Mr. Babcock's room."

"That's where I'm headed, too. Let's go together."

I nodded and stood up. A moment later I had my hand on her arm and we were heading down the hall.

"Here we are," she announced as we came to a stop in front of an open doorway. "I'll meet you at the chess club room at four-thirty. Pete's in my history class, so I can tell him that I'll be walking you home. See you."

She started to walk away and I called out, "Hey, wait a minute," and rushed after her. She stopped and I nearly knocked her down. "What's with this 'I'll walk you home' business?"

"Come on, Hal. I could see how much you wanted to go to the chess club meeting, and it was pretty obvious why you said you couldn't make it. I know Pete takes trumpet on Tuesdays, so it figured you didn't know how you could get home. I live just around the corner from your house, and since I have basketball practice after school tonight it just made sense for us to walk home together."

I didn't know how to react. Sure, I was grateful to her for solving my problem; on the other hand, I resented the way she just assumed I'd want her help. The lure of the chess club won out, however. I muttered my thanks and agreed. But, I assured myself, I wasn't going to let it get to be a habit.

Three

T he room where the chess club met was the old home ec lab in the basement of the school.

"When they built the new lab they turned the old place over to the student union for a club room," Hose told me as we pushed our way through the crowd heading for the exits after the last bell. "It's great for chess — all those sewing tables."

"Are there a lot of members?" I asked, suddenly feeling a little anxious about facing a big group of kids.

"Yeah, chess is big at Churchill. There must be about a hundred regulars and another hundred or so that drop in now and then for a game. Well, here we are." He took my arm and steered me through an open doorway. "There's Marigold; come on, I'll introduce you." Still holding my arm he led me a few feet into the room and stopped.

"Hi there, Hose," a young voice called out. "Been recruiting again?"

"Hi, Marigold. This is Hal Drucker. He's just transferred to Churchill, and he's a chess buff."

"Good to meet you, Hal." She reached out and shook my hand. "Are you beginner, intermediate or expert?"

"Gee, I don't really know. I've never played with anyone but my father and a guy at the school for —" I caught myself and stopped. "At my previous school," I finished. The girl's calm assumption that I could be an expert chess player even though I was blind really blew me away. I wanted desperately to make a good impression, and somehow in my confused mind mentioning that I had attended a school for the blind just wasn't cool.

"Well, I guess the best way to find out how good you are is to set you up with a match. Hose, you're an intermediate. Why don't you take him on? That should give us a pretty good idea where he fits."

When we were seated across the board from each other and we had each made the customary opening moves, I said, "What grade is Marigold in?"

Hose let out a horse laugh and replied, "Marigold is our volunteer instructor. She's married with two kids. Must be over thirty. Pawn to Queen's Bishop Four."

I was stunned. She sounded so young. "Is she good? At chess, I mean. Pawn to King Three."

"The best in the city. Say, are you sure you want to do that?"

"I'm sure."

"Okay." He sounded doubtful as he moved my piece for me. "Knight to King's Bishop Three. Look, do you want me to describe the board to you?"

"I know what the board looks like." Pawn to Queen Four.

Hose continued to chatter away for the next few minutes, then gradually his babbling slowed down until by the eighteenth move he was completely silent.

"Check," I said as I moved my bishop over to Queen Two.

"King to Bishop Four!" Hose said gleefully, just as I knew he would.

"Bishop to King Three: check." I laughed. "Boy, did you ever walk into that one!"

Hose didn't say anything for a minute. Then I heard him tip his king over, signaling that he was resigning. "Are you really that good or was it blind luck?" he asked at last. "Oh, geez, I'm sorry! I didn't mean that."

I laughed again. "Hose, you don't have to apologize for using words like *blind* and *see* and *look*. It's only natural, and half the time I don't even notice. Now, are you ready to get beaten again?"

I took him in twenty moves in the second game. Marigold came over to watch just as I was finishing him off and put her hand on my shoulder.

"Hal, you're really good. Next time I'd like to pit you against our resident expert, Jimmy Chang. He's won the junior inter-city three years in a row."

"There you go bragging again, Marigold," a

voice called from the next table. "I may not be so lucky this year; that new guy over at Bishop Grady is another Bobby Fischer. I played him four times last semester and he won three of the games."

"Come over here, Jimmy," Marigold answered. "I want you to meet our newest expert. Hal, this is Jimmy Chang. Jimmy, Hal Drucker. He just finished Hose off in twenty moves. I'd like to see how he does against you."

A hand reached for mine and shook it.

"Good to meet you, Hal. I need some serious competition. Are you up for a game right now?"

"Sure," I answered eagerly. I was feeling more secure than I had since I left the school for the blind. Here in this club room I'd proved I was able to hold my own; my blindness wasn't a handicap. It was a real high.

I won't bore you with a move by move description of the game. Suffice it to say that at four forty-five when Nancy came looking for me we were still fighting it out. Everyone but Hose and Marigold had left after stopping by our table and watching the match for a moment or two. They all had a teasing remark to make to Jimmy about finally meeting his match and a word of praise for me.

"I think we'd better break this off till next week, fellas," Marigold announced. "I'll copy down the board and you can start where you left off. Unless, of course, you want to finish the game on your own."

"Nah," Jimmy answered before I had a chance to speak. "It can wait."

I had the distinct impression that he was relieved that the game was halted. I wasn't winning, but I wasn't losing either. Maybe it was a little too much for his ego to be seriously challenged by a blind guy.

I said as much to Nancy as we were walking home.

"Come off it, Hal." I couldn't tell if she was angry or just exasperated. "Do you have to relate everything to your blindness?"

"I don't!" I answered hotly. "I just think it's . . . oh, never mind; you wouldn't understand."

"I understand a lot more than you think! Here, we're at your house. Want me to walk to the door with you?"

I was feeling a little twinge of shame for the way I was acting. Nancy had been terrific, and I was treating her like an enemy. "How about coming in for a snack?" I asked. "Mom makes the greatest chocolate chip cookies in the entire country."

"I can't, Hal. I have chores to do and we eat dinner at six."

"Okay. Maybe some other time." I turned abruptly into the path leading to the front door. I didn't want her to see how embarrassed I was. Geez, she probably thought I was coming on to her! So she'd been nice to me; that didn't mean she was interested in somebody who couldn't even find his own way home.

Then just as I reached the top step she called out. "There's a party at Greer Jordon's on Saturday. Want to go?"

I turned in the direction of her voice. "A party? Are you asking me to go to a party with you?"

"That was the general idea." Her voice crackled with amusement. "Greer's birthday is Christmas day, so she always celebrates it after the new year. So, are you interested?"

Sure I was interested. And apprehensive. It sounds impossible, but this would be my first real date with a girl who wasn't blind. All the people I had socialized with before coming home for good were from the school for the blind. It wasn't that I wanted it that way, but that was how it worked out. I was never home long enough to get to know any kids from around here, so I was never invited to any parties. Pete always offered to take me with him, but I never felt comfortable and thought I was an unwelcome responsibility. Now, here was my chance to go to a real party with a normal girl, and I wasn't sure I could handle it.

"I'll take your silence as a yes," Nancy chirped. "See you tomorrow."

When I came through the front door Mom was in the hall waiting for me.

"Hal, dear, are you all right?" Mom's voice was anxious.

"Sure, I'm fine," I answered. "Didn't Pete tell you I would be late?"

"He isn't home yet. It's his trumpet lesson today. I wasn't here when he came home after school. Oh, dear, I've been so worried!"

Even Mom's overprotective attitude couldn't dampen my excitement. "I joined the chess club,

Mom, and I'm really good. At least, that's what
Marigold — she's our instructor — told me. Me
and the top player are in the middle of a match and
I'm really holding my own. It's great."

"That's wonderful, dear. But how did you get
home?"

"A girl I met at school came home with me. She
lives just around the corner." I didn't mention the
party to Mom. I guess I was a little afraid of her
reaction. She'd get all emotional and exaggerate
about how wonderful it was that I was fitting in so
well. Besides, I wasn't entirely sure I was going to
the party. On the one hand, I wanted to get to be
part of a group — to belong. On the other hand, I
was pretty unsure of my ability to cope. I'd talk it
over with Pete before I made up my mind.

"Come on up to your room, dear." Mom put her
hand on my arm. Her voice was filled with excitement. "We have a surprise for you."

I followed her up the stairs, wondering what they
could possibly have got me that I didn't already
have. When I came home before Christmas they'd
had my own phone put in my room, my own TV
and stereo and for Christmas they'd got me a CD
player and a gift certificate for a dozen disks. It was
great to have the stuff, but to be honest, it made me
feel guilty. We're not poor, by any means, but we're
not exactly rolling in it either. Somebody had to do
without so I could be indulged. And I'm afraid the
somebody was Pete, although he never once men-
tioned it.

When we got to my room I could hear a voice

right out of *Star Wars* saying, "Now—is—the—time—for—all—good—men" with a pause after each word.

"What the heck is going on?" I asked as I went into the room.

"Surprise!" Mom and Dad cried in unison.

"It's a computer, son," Dad explained. "A talking computer. Come here and see." He led me over to a new desk and sat me down. "See, you type and it reads back what you've written. It will either repeat each letter as you write it or each word. Or you can program it so it will wait until you finish a sentence then read it back. Isn't that fantastic?"

"Awesome," I whispered. I typed *The quick brown fox* and the mechanical voice repeated the phrase. "Totally awesome." I turned to face them. "But it must have cost an arm and a leg. I don't really need something like this. I record my lectures and Pete helps me with my typing."

"It will make things just that much easier for you, dear," Mom chimed in. "And don't you worry about how much it cost. Nothing is too good for our son."

"Hey, where is everybody?" Pete called out from downstairs.

"We're in Hal's room, Pete. Come up and see what we got for your brother."

A moment later Pete burst into the room. "What is —" He stopped and I heard him gasp. "A computer," he said in a stunned voice.

"It talks," Dad told him, as proud as if he'd built the thing himself.

"Yeah." The bed creaked as Pete sank down on it. His resentment swirled around the room. No one spoke for what seemed like half a day. Then Mom cleared her throat.

"We know how much you've wanted a computer, Pete, but you do understand how much more Hal needs it. Besides, I'm sure you can share it."

Suddenly, I wanted to take that damned smart-ass machine and throw it out the window. Didn't they know how it must have made me feel to be given everything and have Pete get nothing?

Pete must have sensed what I was thinking. He jumped up from the bed and came over to the desk.

"Hey, that's a really terrific machine, Hal. Show me how it works?"

He no longer sounded resentful, only pleased for me.

"I don't know myself yet, Pete. You're the expert. You'll have to show me. And get one thing straight; this computer is as much yours as mine. We'll work out a schedule for when each of us can use it."

"Oh, but —"

I broke in before Mom could finish her protest.

"That's the way it's going to be. We'll put it in the rec room downstairs where we can both use it."

No one argued with me. They never did. That was one good thing about being handicapped.

I think we should give it a name, don't you?" I suggested, trying to lighten the mood.

"Right!" Dad agreed enthusiastically. "How about calling it Gabby?"

"Perfect!" I laughed. It even got a small chuckle out of Pete.

I didn't know very much about computers, but Pete had been using one at school for years. We spent the next hour or so with Pete giving me a crash course on the word-processing program until Mom called us to dinner. Then after dinner I made Pete help me carry the desk with the computer and printer down to the rec room. He protested a lot, but I know he was pleased.

Four

I told Pete about the party as we were walking to school the next day.

"Do you know this Greer person?" I asked, hoping he might give me some idea of the kind of kids I could expect to be there.

"Who doesn't? She's the queen bee of Churchill High. I wish you could see her, Hal. She looks like Cybill Sheppard must have looked when she was sixteen. You know, cool, blond and gorgeous."

"Actually, I don't know, but I'll take your word for it," I answered dryly. Then before he could make the accustomed apology for forgetting I would have no idea what Cybill Sheppard looked like at any age I laughed and said, "Maybe she'll let me check her out in braille."

Pete, relieved that I wasn't going to get sulky, laughed harder than the joke warranted. "Try it and you'll get in big trouble with her boyfriend. Big

Man on Campus type. Football hero, class president and built like a tank."

Football hero? Oh, no! It couldn't be. "What's his name?" I asked, holding my breath.

"Johnny Sterling."

I let my breath out with a whoosh.

"What's the matter? Do you know him?"

"Nope. I just thought it might be a guy I ran into yesterday — literally. I don't think I made a big impression on him. Name's Gord Hadley." I proceeded to tell him about the incident in the hallway and how McGregor embarrassed him in class.

"Oh boy! You picked the wrong guy to cross. He's a jerk, but he carries a lot of weight, what with being on the football team and in the same crowd as Mr. Popularity, Johnny Sterling."

Pete obviously had the same opinion of Gord Hadley as Nancy did, but what did I really know about Nancy? I decided it might be a good idea to find out what he knew about her.

"She's a nice kid," Pete answered. "Everybody's friend type. Smart, too." He paused.

"But?" I prompted.

"Well, she's not exactly centerfold material. Red hair that does its own thing, freckles on her freckles, built like a twelve-year-old boy."

I couldn't help but laugh. "Pete, what she looks like makes no difference to me."

"Yeah, but I'm afraid it does to other people."

We had reached the main foyer, and before I could ask him what he meant, Pete was off down the hall, calling back that he would meet me in the front foyer at four-thirty. He had band practice after school and I was meeting with the counselor to talk about getting some reading on tape done for me.

I shrugged and dismissed the remark as I went off to find my homeroom. I was using my cane and managed to get down the hall without any major calamities and arrived at McGregor's classroom well before the final bell. I was feeling pretty confident as I walked through the door and bumped into a heavy coat. I turned quickly around and apologized. No answer. Then a guffaw.

"Hey, did you see that? The blink just apologized to a coat rack!" Gord Hadley's hated voice came from behind me.

"Knock it off, Gord." It was the girl with the sexy voice from the day before. Then I felt a hand on my arm. "Just ignore him. He's played too many football games without his helmet." I could smell the faint scent of roses as the girl came closer. "My name is Greer Jordon. You're Hal Drucker, aren't you? Pete talks about you all the time. You're his idol."

Needless to say I didn't dazzle her with my quick repartee! Two surprises in one speech was a little too much to handle: first finding out my champion with the voice that made my hands go clammy and my stomach turn cartwheels was the famous Greer Jordon, then hearing that Pete called me his idol. I didn't need to worry, though. Greer carried on without apparently noticing my inability to form simple sentences.

"Nancy tells me you'll be coming to my birthday party on Saturday. I'm so pleased."

"Uh, yeah, sure," I blurted out. "I'm looking forward to it."

"So am I." She released my arm and walked away.

I managed to stumble to my seat without accosting any more inanimate objects and sank down, still slightly awed by what had happened. A moment later Mr. McGregor came into the room and the day began in earnest.

Nancy picked me up at the science lab again that noon and walked with me to the cafeteria. I could have made it on my own, but I was glad she showed up. It's not much fun eating alone.

Hose joined us at the large table in the middle of the room where Nancy had found the last three seats. He organized my meal without making a big production of it and began his non-stop monologue.

"Where did you learn to play chess, Hal? You must have been playing since you were in kindergarten to get so good, or are you just a natural? Hey, everybody." His voice rose as he commanded the attention of the whole table. "You should have seen this guy take on Jimmy Chang yesterday. He's incredible!"

There was a murmur of voices, then someone spoke out. "You play chess? But how can you keep track of where all the pieces are?"

"I keep a picture of the board in my head. It's not so difficult really."

"Not for you, maybe," someone else commented," but I can't even remember my own postal code!"

Laughter, then a third voice. "Is it true that when you lose your sight your other senses get stronger?"

"I suppose so, but it's not automatic. You work to develop your other senses to compensate. For instance, I rely a lot on my ears to give me clues about my environment, but my hearing isn't any more acute than anyone else's. I just pay more attention to it."

At first I was embarrassed by the personal questions. Then I found I was enjoying myself. The kids seemed genuinely interested in me, and they certainly weren't acting uncomfortable about talking to me about my handicap.

"I saw this movie once about a guy who was blind — something about butterflies. He was able to sense when he was coming near a wall or a door or furniture — stuff like that. Can you do it?"

I laughed. "I guess I can sometimes, but mostly I rely on the cane to tell me what's ahead of me. And even then I spend a lot of time walking into things like low-hanging tree branches. And I'm always apologizing to inanimate objects," I added for the benefit of anyone who might have seen my conversation with the coat rack that morning.

Gradually the conversation returned to the basketball team's chances of winning the girls' quarter finals on the weekend and the upcoming Valentine dance.

When everyone seemed to be busy talking to everyone else Nancy leaned across the table and spoke. "The party starts at eight o'clock. Want me to come by for you about ten to?"

"Yeah, sure, that would be fine," I answered.

"Hey, Nancy!" A voice called out. "You got yourself a date? Well, hallelujah! Will wonders never cease."

It was the hated voice of Gord Hadley. He was apparently passing the table when Nancy was speaking to me and overheard her.

There were a few subdued giggles from the other end of the table, then Hose said angrily, "Shut up, Hadley. No one's interested in your juvenile comments."

Dead silence, then Hadley, furious and threatening, responded, "Yeah? And who's gonna make me?"

I felt an arm reach out beside me and Hose's chair suddenly fell over.

"Look, fella, I don't know what your problem is, but I've just about had it with your sick attitude." I felt the same red-hot anger flowing over me as I had when I'd decked The Goon at the school for the blind, and I was all psyched up to punch the guy out.

"Well, get him," Gord answered with a short humorless laugh. "And just what are you planning to do about it, blink? Beat me with your white cane?"

"Okay, knock it off, Gord," somebody else said. "You're making a fool of yourself."

The arm retreated and I heard Hose pick up his chair and sit down.

"Okay, Johnny," Hadley said, "but no little pip-squeak is gonna tell me to shut up and get away with it. I'll see you later, pipsqueak." This last remark was obviously directed to Hose. He had apparently chosen to ignore me.

My anger faded and I began to think about what Gord had said to Nancy. I was disgusted with him for his cruel remark, but I couldn't help wondering if he was just saying what everyone else thought. My mind went back to that morning and Pete's enigmatic comment about Nancy when I said I didn't care what she looked like. Was she a loser? Someone who couldn't get a date? Was I just a last resort? Was I jeopardizing my chances of being accepted by getting involved with her? The questions swirled around in my head unanswered.

Nancy must have sensed what was going on in my head. She got up and came around to my side of the table. "Come on, let's go," she suggested, taking my arm. Then, when we were alone in the hall, she said, "Look, Hal, if you don't want to go to Greer's party with me, just say so. But please don't think I asked you because I felt sorry for you, or," she added grimly, "because I couldn't get anyone else. I really like you and I think we could have a lot of fun together."

Shame covered me like a thick coarse blanket — uncomfortable and suffocating. Here was a girl who had gone all out to be my friend, and I was worried about what a sleaze like Hadley thought of her.

"Of course I want to go to the party with you. Do you want me to arrange a ride?"

I could hear her sigh of relief. "No, that's okay. I've got my own car." She started to leave and I suddenly remembered that it was a birthday party.

"Wait, Nancy. What are you giving Greer?"

"Why? You don't need to bring anything. You don't even know her, and I'm sure she won't expect anything from you."

No way, I thought to myself. But what could I give her? Then I remembered the scent of roses I'd detected when she came up to me. I'd ask Mom what kind of perfume smelled like roses and get some for her.

After assuring Nancy I could find my way to my next class I left her in the hall and headed for Mr. Babcock's room and math 200.

Five

The rest of the day went by without anything very earthshaking happening. I started getting a fix on who was in my various classes and found to my great relief that Hadley wasn't in most of them. Unfortunately, neither was Greer Jordon. Nancy and I didn't have any classes together, so I didn't see her again until I was waiting for Pete at the end of the day. I had decided I'd ask Mom to take me shopping for Greer's perfume as soon as we got home and was shifting impatiently from foot to foot when she stopped beside me.

"Hey, you're still here, Hal. Ready to go home?" She took my hand and started to put it on her arm. "If it's okay with you I'll take you up on that chocolate chip cookie offer."

"Well, actually, Nancy," I fumbled, moving away, "I'm waiting for Pete."

"Okay, we'll wait together."

I began to feel the anger well up inside me. I liked Nancy and I was very appreciative of all the help she'd given me, but I didn't like the way she was taking control of my life. I had had enough of that at the school for the blind. She had no right to assume that I'd have no plans for after school and that naturally I'd be grateful for her company.

"Look, Nancy, I'm going to be busy."

"Oh, I see. Well, maybe another time." She sounded hurt, or maybe it was embarrassment I heard in her voice. At any rate, the anger I was feeling disappeared and I began to feel sorry for the way I was acting. I really did want to get the perfume, though, and today would be the only chance I'd have. Mom worked the eleven-to-seven shift at the hospital, and her days off were Tuesday and Wednesday.

"Sure, that would be great," I answered. "How about tomorrow?"

"That's cool." I heard the smile return to her voice. "Well, I'd better get going. Sure you don't want me to wait with you until Pete shows up? The place is getting kind of deserted."

"No, I'll be fine." I'm not a two-year-old who needs his mommy to stay with him, I wanted to add, but I kept my mouth shut. I heard her walk away, and then silence. She's only trying to be helpful, I reminded myself. You've got to stop being so darned sensitive. But it wasn't easy.

I leaned back against the office door and checked my watch. Four-forty. Pete was late. I began pacing up and down in front of the office, wondering what to do, when the door suddenly opened and I crashed into a tiny person swathed in fur.

"Oops, excuse me," a woman I recognized as the school secretary said. "Were you wanting something, young man? I'm just about to lock up for the night."

"No, that's okay," I mumbled and backed away. "Sorry I ran into you."

"Think nothing of it." I heard the key turn in the lock and her footsteps as she walked toward the exit. Another ten minutes passed and no Pete. I began to panic. Something had happened. He wasn't going to show up. Maybe band got out early. Or had I got the time wrong. What would I do?

Call Mom. She'd come and get me. But how? The office was locked and I didn't know where or even *if* there was a pay phone. If only I hadn't turned down Nancy's offer to stay with me. I'd walked home from school only twice before and always with someone. I thought I knew the way, but I wasn't dead sure. Then there was that busy crossing at Grant Avenue and Fourteenth Street. It scared me even when someone was with me.

I waited another five minutes, hoping Pete had just been delayed or that someone would come along I could ask to phone home for me. The foyer remained deserted.

At five o'clock I knew I'd have to do something. I couldn't stay in the school all night. But what?

Then it hit me; I was getting spaced out over nothing. Pete would come home without me, and Mom would realize I must still have been in the

school. She would come for me. I walked over to
the heavy front door and shoved it open to listen.
Then from somewhere behind me I heard footsteps.

"Okay, fella, you'll have to leave now," a gruff
voice called. "I'm locking up for the night."

I turned quickly. "But I . . ."

"Now don't give me no static. I said, leave." He
took me by the arm and before I knew what was
happening I was out the door and on the front steps
of the school.

I turned and pounded on the door, but the custodian either didn't hear me or had decided I was just
some nut best ignored. I'd put my white cane away
in my book bag as soon as I'd made my way to the
foyer, so there was no way he could know I was
blind. I was just another nuisance kid. I flopped
against the door and shivered. It was getting cold.
I couldn't stand around waiting for someone to
come for me. No one knew where I was, and until
Pete came home Mom wouldn't realize anything
was wrong. I had only one choice. I'd have to find
my way back to the house on my own.

I walked down the school steps, found the sidewalk with no problem and proceeded south up the
street. I wasn't using my cane and when I came to
the corner I fell off the curb and landed in an
undignified heap in the gutter. Embarrassed and
feeling really stupid, I tried to hear if there was
anyone in the immediate vicinity who might have
seen me, then pulled the hated cane out of my book
bag. I crossed Thirteenth Street and continued on

to the next intersection with nothing more disastrous happening than walking into a low-hanging
branch and giving myself a whack on the forehead.
At Fourteenth Street I turned east and walked the
block to Grant Avenue.

At five o'clock the rush-hour traffic is almost
bumper to bumper. I could hear it roaring past me
coming from both directions. Grant and Fourteenth
is a controlled intersection, but there's a turning
lane on Grant, where cars can advance on the red.
I stood on the curb, waiting to hear the traffic on
Grant come to a halt so I could cross, but when it
did I was afraid to move. The traffic passed beside
me on Fourteenth, then the cars in the right lane on
Grant began whizzing around the corner.

The lights changed again and I stood paralyzed,
my cane at my side, as I listened to the cars moving
along Grant. When they stopped and I heard the
cars start up again on Fourteenth I forced myself
to put my cane up and take a tentative step off the
curb. A car, apparently not seeing me, swept
around the corner from Grant and I had to jump
back onto the sidewalk to avoid getting hit. I was
so shaken that I could barely stand up. I walked
over to the edge of the sidewalk and leaned against
a building, trying to stop the trembling that had
taken over my whole body.

I'd been standing there for what seemed like
hours but was probably only a minute or two when
I felt a hand on my arm.

"Can I help you, son?" a man said beside me.

I nodded, unable to speak. I'd never been so

scared in my life. Sure, I'd been taught at the school for the blind how to cope in traffic, but the traffic in the town where the school was located was nothing like here. And added to my fear was my embarrassment at being helpless.

"Where did you want to go?" he asked, taking me by the arm.

"Across Grant Avenue," I managed to answer.

Without another word he began steering me down the curb and across the traffic. I staggered along beside him, hoping I wouldn't stumble and fall in the middle of the road. The man was trying to be helpful, but he sure didn't know how to lead a blind person. Instead of letting me hold his arm he was pulling at mine, half leading, half carrying me across the street.

Eventually we made it to the other side without disaster. I turned to thank him, pulling my arm from his clutches, but he was not to be dismissed so easily. He gripped my arm tighter and said, "Now where can I take you?"

"I'm okay," I assured him. "My house is just a block down the street. I can make it from here."

"Nonsense!" He began to walk in the direction I'd pointed, still pulling me along behind him. If it hadn't been so infuriating, it would have been funny.

"Which house is yours?" he asked as we neared the corner.

"Last house on the block," I answered, hoping he would give me back my arm. But he wasn't about to surrender me so easily.

"I'll just see that you get in safely," he said, and

without further comment he had me through the gate, up the front stairs and was ringing the door-bell.

"Oh, Hal!" Mom cried when she opened the door and saw me standing there with my rescuer. "What happened to you?"

"Found him down at the corner trying to cross the street," the man answered for me. "Name's Gross. Shouldn't be out alone. The boy, I mean. Well, I'd better be on my way. Take care, young man, and don't let me find you wandering around in traffic by yourself again."

"Th-thank you, Mr., ah . . ." Mom stuttered. Then, taking my arm, she led me into the house.

"What happened, Hal? Why isn't Pete with you?" Mom asked again as she sat me down at the kitchen table.

"I don't know. I thought we were supposed to meet at four-thirty. I guess I must have got the time or the place wrong. Isn't he home yet?"

"No, he —" She was interrupted by the front door opening and Pete calling out.

"Anybody home?" A moment later he came roaring into the kitchen. "Hi, everybody," he said. "Guess what? I've been made lead trumpet in the band. Isn't that wild? Jason Harvey thought he'd get it — everybody did — but Mrs. Nabors gave it to me." He flopped down beside me and blew out his breath.

"Where have you been, Peter?" Mom's voice was cold steel.

"We went to Jimmy's Ribs to celebrate," he

answered. "Oh, man! You can't believe how —"

"And left your brother to find his own way home. How very considerate."

Mom is usually the best-natured person in the world; I don't think I've ever heard her utter a sarcastic word. It was a shock.

"Oh, my God!" Pete exclaimed, and his chair fell to the ground as he jumped to his feet. "I totally forgot. The promotion and all. I guess I . . ." The words faded and he caught his breath.

"You forgot! You're responsible for seeing your blind brother gets home without killing himself in traffic and you forgot!"

All the fear and frustration of the past hour disappeared, and I wanted nothing more than to shut Mom up. "Look, it's no big deal," I said. "I got home okay — no problem. It was a perfectly natural thing for Pete to forget. After all, it's not every day a guy gets promoted to first trumpet."

It was no use. She was far too angry and probably scared to let it rest. "Well, just to help you remember your responsibilities I'm grounding you for two weeks. You'll come home right after school and you won't go out again until the next morning. Now go to your room. I'll call you when dinner's ready."

Pete got up without a word and left the room.

"Mom, don't be so upset," I pleaded. "Pete didn't mean any harm."

"Oh, Hal!" She sounded as though she was crying. "Don't you understand? You could have been run over; that man who brought you home could have been a criminal; you could have gotten lost or fallen and broken something." I heard her swallow a sob, then she murmured, "I should have gone looking for you myself."

I couldn't take it any longer. Her anger at Pete was bad enough, but I just couldn't hack that guilty sound that crept into her voice every time something went the least little bit wrong for me. I got up from the table and stomped out of the room.

I found Pete in his room lying on the bed and playing his stereo.

"Pete, I'm really sorry about getting you into trouble. I never would have told Mom anything, but this guy insisted on bringing me home and making a big production of rescuing me."

"No, it's me who should be sorry, Hal. I never should have gotten so carried away about the stupid band thing." I heard him turn over and his voice was muffled as he added, "Don't worry. It won't happen again."

I left him lying there and went to my own room, feeling like I wanted to hit something. I went around touching the stereo and CD player, the TV that I couldn't even see, my own phone. And I thought of the expensive computer the folks had bought me. Pete had none of this stuff, and as an added bonus he was expected to arrange his life to accommodate me. It wasn't fair — not to him, not to me. If only I hadn't decked the phys ed teacher, both of us would probably have been a lot better off.

Six

I told Nancy the next day at lunch what had happened. I know that sounds strange, but I had to talk to someone and it couldn't be my family. They were too close to the problem. I was afraid she would make some crack about how it never would have happened if I hadn't sent her packing, but she didn't. Instead, she gave me a mini-lecture on how to cope as a blind person.

"Hal, you've got to learn to be independent. You can't always expect Pete or your folks to be around to watch over you."

"Geez, Nancy, do you think I don't know that?"

"Yes, I do think exactly that. You're so hung up on being quote normal unquote that you do stupid things that get you into trouble. Like not using your cane, for instance. And did it ever occur to you to ask for help when you're not sure of yourself?"

I muttered that there'd been no one to ask yesterday, and was about to argue that I *was* using my cane when I remembered I'd put it out of sight in my book bag.

"Have you ever thought of a seeing-eye dog, Hal? My grandfather has one, and he says it's almost as good as having your own eyes."

"No way!" I exclaimed. "It's bad enough that I have to draw attention to myself with the cane. A dog is out of the question."

She let out a deep sigh. "That's just stupid, but if you're so determined to pretend you're not blind, then at least learn to find your way around."

"And just what does that mean?" I was wishing I'd kept my mouth shut about the fiasco. I expected sympathy and understanding, not an inventory of my faults.

"You need to be able to walk home alone, for starters. Now, hold it just a minute," she said as I started to interrupt. "I know the crossing at Grant Avenue and Fourteenth Street is wild, but you don't have to take that route. You could cross Grant a block earlier at Thirteenth. It's a very quiet street. There's no stoplight, but there's a pedestrian crosswalk. All you'd have to do is put your cane out in front of you and the cars would stop. You wouldn't have to worry about someone coming around the corner, and you'd be able to hear the traffic a lot better."

"I doubt that would solve my problem," I muttered, thinking she was way out in left field. Cross without a light? It sounded like a good way to commit suicide!

"I think it would." The warning bell for afternoon classes rang, and I picked up my books, wanting to get away from her and her great schemes. "Will you just give it a try? I'll meet you after school and we'll test it out." Without waiting for me to protest she stood up and, after pushing her chair back, walked away.

* * *

I was feeling so great when school ended that I forgot all about Nancy.

First, I'd aced a math test and Mr. Babcock had made a big deal of it in class.

"It's not every day I see a perfect algebra paper," he said. "I just hope Mr. Drucker proves to be an example to all of you of what can be done with a little effort."

The second thing that had made my day happened during study period. I was just sitting down with my tape recorder and earphone to go over some notes when Jimmy Chang tapped me on the shoulder.

"Want to finish our game, Drucker?" he asked.

I was more than a little surprised. I'd thought Jimmy was avoiding the game. Besides, how could we play chess during school hours?

He must have read my mind. "It's okay. I got permission from Mrs. Griffiths. Our principal is a big chess fan, you know. I told her I needed the practice if I was going to beat the guy over at Bishop Grady. The truth is I've been dying to finish our game — find out if you're always as good as the other day or if that was just a fluke."

To make a long story short, we played and I won.

It took the whole hour to beat him, but I did it.

I told Hose about the game during the next period, phys ed. I'm not expected to take part in any of the games, but when we do calisthenics I have to participate. Hose had sprained his ankle the day before, walking his dog (he admitted he was a tad accident-prone, this being the third sprain in as many months), so he was sitting in the stands with me.

"Hal, that's incredible! Nobody beats Jimmy Chang unless he gives them an advantage." Then, before I could stop him he was on his feet calling to the guys on the benches beside us who were waiting for their turn on the volleyball court. "Hey, listen up. Hal here just took Jimmy Chang in an even game. No handicaps. Isn't that awesome?"

I couldn't believe anyone would really care one way or another about a chess match, but I'd forgotten how big the game was at Churchill. In fact, it was big in most of the high schools in the city, and the upcoming tournament was a major event.

"Hey, that's great," a guy a few rows down said. "We sure need more strength on the team. Jimmy's been carrying us almost alone for the past year."

A few more guys called out their congratulations, then the teacher shouted for everyone to get down on the floor for a few laps around the gym before the end of the period, and Hose and I were left alone.

"You're sure to be asked to be on the school team, Hal," Hose assured me as we headed for the locker room. "You can do just about anything you want to, can't you? Do you think it's harder to be deaf or blind? I'd think deaf. You'd feel so out of it if you couldn't hear. Do you dream in pictures?"

I wasn't sure which question to answer, so I tackled the last one. "Sure, I dream in pictures. Don't forget I was able to see until I was seven years old. I can remember what things looked like. But even people who have been blind since birth often dream in pictures; it must be their mind's version of what things look like, I guess. It's strange and I don't know what they see in their dreams, but lots of guys at the school for the blind told me they do it."

"That's really weird. I wonder if they picture people looking like elephants and flowers looking like tables?"

Fortunately, a shower stall came empty before I had to field *that* one!

* * *

When Nancy showed up at three-thirty while I was waiting for Pete in the front foyer it took me a minute to remember why she was there.

"Ready to go?" she asked. "Pete'll be along in a couple of minutes. He said to go without him; he'd catch up."

She took my arm and, paying no attention to my protests, led me out the door and down the steps. At the bottom she removed her hand and stepped away from me. "Now you're on your own, Hal. I'll be right behind you, but you'll have to walk by yourself."

I started to protest, then, realizing it would do no

good, pulled out my cane and started up the street.
I used the cane as I'd been taught to do at the
school, moving it back and forth ahead of me, and
managed to get to the corner without a calamity.
As I turned on Thirteenth Street and headed over
to Grant, I heard Pete call out from behind me and
Nancy explain what was going on.

"He can't cross Grant by himself," Pete protested.

"Sure he can," Nancy answered. "Besides, nothing can happen to him. We're right here."

"Mom'll kill me if she finds out," Pete muttered,
but he didn't make any attempt to stop me.

When I reached Grant I could hear the cars
roaring by. It wasn't rush hour, but it was still
plenty busy. I stood on the sidewalk for a moment,
then, putting my cane straight out in front of me, I
stepped off the curb. I could hear the cars on my
left come to a halt, but I was afraid to start across.
Visions of someone coming from the other direction and smearing me onto the pavement ran
through my head. Then a woman's gentle voice
came from the car nearest me.

"It's okay, young man. The traffic has stopped.
You can cross now."

I hesitated for a second, then took the plunge. A
moment later I was stepping safely onto the opposite curb and the traffic started up behind me. I let
out a huge sigh of relief and grinned.

Crossing Thirteenth was no problem, and since
we lived on the north side of Fourteenth I didn't

have any more streets to cross. I was home in another five minutes.

"See, I told you you could do it," Nancy gloated as she and Pete joined me at the front of our house. "Now the next assignment is to get you using the bus."

I was feeling like I'd just won a lottery as we went into the house together. I wasn't sure it was from pride over making the trip alone or relief that it was over and I still had all my parts. At that moment I felt I could handle anything.

"Sure," I answered Nancy as we went into the house and headed for the kitchen. "When do you want to go for it?"

"How about Saturday afternoon? The buses won't be so crowded and the traffic should be lighter."

I hesitated for just a moment, wondering if I was taking things too quickly. Then I remembered Greer's birthday present. I figured I needed a woman to help me pick it out, and I knew Mom wouldn't be able to take me shopping. Although she didn't have to be at work until eleven on Saturday, she had her aerobics class at nine and then had her hair done. There was no way I was going to ask her to cancel either of them for me.

"You're on," I agreed. "Can we go to a mall?"

"Sure. I'll come over around two." She sat down beside me at the kitchen table and spoke to Pete, who was busy getting stuff out of the fridge. "How about coming with us?" she asked.

"No!" he shouted, slamming the fridge door and banging dishes down on the table. I felt Nancy stiffen. "I've got other plans," he added in a quieter voice.

"Suit yourself." She sounded surprised and a little annoyed.

"Wait'll you try one of Mom's cookies," I said, trying to break the tension that was threatening to smother us. Pete couldn't go to the mall, of course. Because of me he'd been grounded. But he obviously wasn't going to explain that to Nancy, and I knew if I tried it would make him even angrier. The familiar feeling of being an unavoidable burden washed over me.

The charged atmosphere lasted another couple of minutes, then Nancy said, "I hear you beat Jimmy Chang today. Word's out all over school that you're going to be invited to play on the school team."

I shrugged and muttered something unintelligible.

"Hey, that's great, Hal." Pete sounded genuinely enthusiastic. And no longer angry. I didn't, I told myself, deserve a brother like him.

The tension had broken, and we went on to talk about various school activities, teachers, upcoming parties — the usual stuff high school kids talk about, I guess.

Nancy left shortly afterward, and Pete began clearing up the table. "Here, let me help," I offered, reaching for the plate of cookies. My arm brushed against the milk jug, and before I could grab it the milk was flowing all over the table. I heard Pete sigh.

"Never mind, Hal. I'll take care of it." He snatched the upset pitcher and walked over to the sink. I got up and left the room.

Lying on my bed a few minutes later, I played the scene in the kitchen over and over in my mind. Pete had every right to be mad at me for causing him to be grounded. He had every right to be mad at me for a lot of things. But he never seemed to get angry. That was the first time I'd ever seen him lose control, and although he recovered real quick, it was obvious from the way he acted when I spilled the milk he was still pretty damn fed up with me. Always before he's made a big joke if I spilled anything.

I rolled over and closed my eyes. Why kid myself, I thought. I may have been his idol once, as Greer had pointed out, but that was when I was hundreds of miles away. Now he was stuck with me and it wasn't turning out to be any picnic.

Seven

When I awoke on Saturday morning I could tell no one was up yet. The house was so quiet that I could hear the fridge defrosting. I felt my watch and discovered it was a little before seven. I turned over and tried to go back to sleep but it was no use. I was far too wound up thinking about the trip to the mall with Nancy and the party at Greer's in the evening.

I got up and slipped quietly out to the kitchen where I made myself a cheese sandwich. Then, taking my dry breakfast downstairs, I went into the rec room and started the computer. A half hour later I'd finished the essay on the invasion of Poland I'd been assigned for Mr. McGregor's class and went back upstairs to see if anyone had managed to come to life yet.

I heard Mom at the stove frying bacon and Dad at the table drinking coffee and shuffling the morning paper. There was no sign of Pete.

"I guess he's sulking in his room," Mom answered when I asked about him. "Some girl called him last night — something about a skating party. He wanted to go pretty badly, but of course he's been grounded."

My stomach did a flip-flop. Pete would be even more put off with me. I wanted to go upstairs and tell him how sorry I was for causing him so much trouble, but I knew instinctively that would be the wrong thing to do. Instead, I forced myself to eat the bacon and eggs Mom put in front of me, and as soon as I could escape I went to my room and shut the door. I stayed there listening to a book on tape and fooling with some chess moves until a little before two when I heard the doorbell ring.

* * *

The trip to the Village Square Mall was much easier than I'd expected. The bus stop was at the corner of Thirteenth and Grant, an easy walk from the house. Nancy coached me on what to do when the bus came and I had no trouble getting on and off without her help. She also made me count the stops the bus made so I would know when to get off if I went by myself. Fat chance, I thought, but I humored her anyway.

While we were riding along Nancy began to talk about her grandfather, the one who was blind. "He's terrific," she told me. "He lost his sight during the Second World War, but it didn't stop him from coming home and getting a law degree."

"That's what I want to do," I remarked. "Be a

lawyer, I mean. I don't know if I'll make it; it won't be easy."

"No, it won't, but you can do anything you want, Hal. That's what Grampa says."

"You really care a lot about your grandfather, don't you?"

"He's the greatest. He's not only real smart but he has a fabulous sense of humor." She started to laugh. "One time he was out walking with my grandmother and his hand, which was dangling at his side, suddenly touched fur. He thought it was a dog, so he bent down and patted it. Only it turned out to be a women in a fur coat tying her shoelace."

"God, he must have wanted to die of embarrassment."

"On the contrary," she replied, still laughing, "I think he's told that story to everyone he's ever met."

The guy must be a little strange, I thought, but I didn't say anything to Nancy. Let her think her grandfather is a real hero.

We got off the bus shortly and walked half a block or so to the parking lot in front of the mall. Crossing it to the mall entrance was a little more challenging, but I made it on my own, with Nancy following a few feet behind, of course.

"See how easy that was?" she gloated as we walked though the doors together. "Now, where do you want to go?"

"First, let's get something to eat," I suggested. "I didn't have any lunch."

"Okay by me. I can always eat."

She led the way to the Food Fair, where we loaded up on burgers and fries and took them to a semi-isolated table at the far corner of the room. We didn't try to talk until we'd demolished most of the food and were sipping our shakes. Then Nancy opened the conversation.

"What was it like living at the school for the blind?" she asked, sucking the last bit of liquid through her straw with a loud gurgling sound.

"Safe," I answered with a grin.

"No, really. What were the kids like?"

"Most of them were pretty normal except for their vision. Then there were the ISs."

"ISs?"

"Yeah. Idiot savants. About a third of the population was mentally handicapped as well as blind. And out of that group there were a few that were totally hopeless except in one area where they were practically geniuses."

"For instance?"

"Well, there was Lamoine Pipkin who could play the piano like Horowitz but thought he was a John Deere tractor."

"You made that up!"

"No, honestly. He used to go out into the schoolyard and run up and down plowing the field and clapping his hands in that peculiar rhythm tractors have. The only way you could stop him was to get behind him, twist his overalls and say, 'Your key's turned off, Lamoine.' Then he'd slow down gradually until the gas stopped flowing into the engine."

Nancy let out a guffaw that sprayed the last of her shake across the table and got me in the chin. "Oh, I'm sorry," she sputtered, reaching over and wiping my face with a napkin. "Is that really true?"

"Scout's honor. Then there was Kermit, the lock picker. He could pick any lock ever invented. We used to take him with us to the pantry at night, and he'd open up the door so we could load up on stuff to eat. They kept changing the locks, but it didn't stop Kermit. It was just as well he had that talent. He couldn't find his way from his room to the dining hall, and unless someone took him by the hand he'd end up in the laundry room or the principal's bathroom and miss dinner."

"You all ate together, then?"

"Yeah," I groaned, "dictated by bells. There was the bell to wash up, then the bell to gather in the outer foyer and wait, then the bell to go into the dining hall and finally the bell to eat. It was because of those damn bells that I got expelled the first time. At the end of the meal a bell sounded for the girls to leave. The guys had to wait another ten minutes for their bell. I figured it was stupid, so one night I organized the guys to leave with the girls. I was sent to the principal's office, of course, and told to apologize to the dining room supervisor for disobeying the rules. I wouldn't, so they kicked me out."

"They expelled you?"

"Yeah, but Dad managed to get me reinstated. The next time I was expelled — this was just before Christmas — they wouldn't take me back. That's why I'm here now."

"And are you glad you left the school and came to Churchill?"

"I guess so, but I still feel pretty unsure of myself a lot of the time."

"You'll get over that once you get to know more kids. The party tonight should help that along."

"Yeah, about the party. Who all will be there?"

"Mostly just Greer's close friends — and Johnny Sterling's buddies, I suppose."

I felt my throat tighten and my mouth go dry. "Does that mean Gord Hadley will be there?"

"Well —" she hesitated " — yes, I guess it does. But don't worry about him, Hal. Nobody takes him seriously."

Maybe not, I thought, but he sure makes me feel like a schmuck. I didn't admit it to Nancy, though. Instead, I tried to change the subject to something much more pleasant.

"So how long have you known Greer?" I asked.

"We've been best friends since kindergarten. All through elementary school we were inseparable, then she suddenly turned into Miss America and every boy with normal hormones swarmed around her. I, on the other hand —" she laughed ruefully "— am still waiting for the big transformation. We're still very close friends, but we don't spend as much time together as we used to."

"Has she been going with Johnny Sterling for long?"

"Since the beginning of Grade 10. It was really

hot for a while, but I think she's cooling off a little on him. I suppose it's just as well; he'll be going away to university next year."

I could feel my whole face light up. "Really? That's interesting."

Nancy didn't speak for a moment. "Yes, isn't it?" she replied in an odd tone. Then she continued briskly. "Okay, now where do you want to go?"

"I'd like to pick up a birthday gift for Greer," I answered somewhat hesitantly. "I know you said I didn't need to, but I'd feel dumb going to the party without one."

"Sure. What did you have in mind?"

"I thought some perfume. Something that smells like roses."

Nancy got up and came around the table to take my arm. "Okay. We'll go to The Bay. They've got a good selection."

A few minutes later we were standing at the perfume counter and Nancy was looking through the sample bottles.

"Here, smell this," she ordered, squirting a little on my wrist.

I took a whiff and grinned. "That's perfect! How does it come?"

"You can get either perfume or cologne, spray or regular." Something in her voice sounded peculiar, but I paid little attention. I was so pleased that I'd found exactly the right stuff.

"Which do you think I should get?" I asked, sniffing my wrist again.

"Well, that depends on how much you want to

spend. The perfume is a hundred and twenty for the spray, ninety-five for the regular. That's for a quarter ounce. Now the cologne is cheaper. It costs only seventy-five —"

"Dollars?" I cried, dropping her arm like it was a loaded gun.

"No, yen. Of course dollars. You don't think this stuff comes cheap, do you?"

I didn't say anything. I just stood there feeling stupid. Finally Nancy laughed. "I'm sorry, Hal. I was putting you on. That's the most expensive perfume in the store. Come on, let's check out the soaps. You can get a really nice box of Pink Roses for about five bucks." Taking my hand, she placed it on her arm again and led me down the aisle.

We bought the soap and then wandered around the mall while Nancy checked out all the shoe and clothing sales. At four o'clock we stopped at an ice-cream stand for sundaes. Nancy had bought a new skirt and sweater to wear to the party that night and had talked me into buying a blue sweater and a pair of socks to match.

"Wear it with those great dark gray cords you had on last Tuesday," she ordered. "They'll look terrific together."

I couldn't understand her. She was being so great about helping me with everything from getting around independently to coordinating my clothes. Yet she'd pulled that stunt at the perfume counter. She must have known I'd be embarrassed. It didn't figure.

I was still pondering it when we arrived at my house an hour later.

"Want to come in?" I asked.

"Nope. I've gotta get home and make myself beautiful."

"Okay, see you later." I dropped my hand from her arm and turned into the path leading to the front door.

"Right," she called after me, "and don't forget the blue sweater. And," she added quietly, "the soap."

Eight

*T*he minute we walked into the huge rumpus room where the party was being held I knew I shouldn't have come. The noise was deafening. Rock music blasted from all four corners of the room; voices shrieked above it. I was totally disoriented as I always am in a crowd. Nancy seemed unaware of my discomfort, however. After pausing for the briefest moment in the doorway, she took my arm and led me into the middle of the mob.

"Hi, Nancy, Hal. Glad you could make it," the voice that made my tongue go numb murmured, and Greer slipped her hand in mine. "Come on and meet some of the kids."

"Um, this is for you," I mumbled, handing her the box of soap I'd had gift-wrapped at the store.

"Why, Hal, how sweet, but you didn't need to bring me a present." She took the gift and began leading me through the crowd. Nancy dropped my arm and followed a step or two behind.

We stopped in front of a group of people, and Greer began introductions. "Johnny, this is Hal Drucker. He's just transferred to Churchill from . . . ?" She paused and waited for me to fill in the blank.

"Back east," I hedged. "Nice to meet you."

"You too." He reached out and took my hand, the one Greer wasn't holding. I felt like I was being gripped by a gorilla. By the size of his hand I judged Greer's boyfriend to be about six foot six. I'm six feet myself, but he must have towered over me.

"Well, look who's here? Nancy and her bl —" The voice coming from the right of Johnny was unmistakably that of Gord Hadley. I guess I must have involuntarily stiffened because Greer broke in quickly before he could finish.

"Hal, you know Gord Hadley, and this is his girlfriend, Rona Riley. Would you like something to drink?" she rushed on. "The punch bowl is just over this way."

"Why don't you crawl back in your hole and pull it over your head, Gordon Hadley," I heard Nancy hiss as we moved away from Johnny and his friends.

As soon as we were out of earshot Greer said, "Don't pay any attention to Gord. He's annoying but harmless."

I wasn't so sure of that, but I didn't say anything. Holding Greer's hand made even Gord Hadley's presence almost tolerable.

After Greer poured me a glass of punch she excused herself to meet a couple that was just arriving. Nancy moved closer to me and mumbled, "You can wipe that silly grin off your face now. She's gone."

I felt the blood rush to my face, and I turned away from her muttering, "I wasn't aware I was wearing a silly grin," with an emphasis on the last two words.

"Well, you were." She sounded hurt. "I guess you want to know what Greer looks like, eh?"

"Doesn't make any difference to me," I lied. I wanted to find out everything about her — Pete's description had been totally useless — but I wasn't going to let Nancy know how I felt.

"Whatever," she replied noncomittally. "Want to dance?"

"In this crowd?"

"No, I thought we'd go out on the lawn! Of course in this crowd." She grabbed my drink and deposited it on the table. Then, taking my hand, she dragged me over to the other end of the room where the rug had been taken up for dancing.

It was awful. I can dance just fine if I'm holding a girl, but when I have to dance by myself it's a total disaster. I kept losing track of Nancy and wandering off on my own, much to the amusement of the kids around me. I bumped into people and stepped on people's feet. I felt like the proverbial bull in a china shop. Nancy paid no attention to my floundering — she just kept on dancing. I figured she was getting back at me for drooling over Greer.

It was finally dawning on me why she had acted so strangely at the perfume counter. It seemed hard to believe, but I was beginning to think she was jealous. If I hadn't been so angry with her I would have been flying high. For the first time in my life a girl was jealous of another girl over me! I admit it would have been better if it had been Greer who was jealous, but it was still a big turn-on.

The tape finally ended and Nancy returned to my side. The music didn't start up again, so we went back to the punch table and filled our glasses. A moment later Greer's voice came from the front of the room.

"Listen up, everybody. We're going to play a couple of games."

A low voice came from a few feet away. "I hope it's not blind man's buff."

A few titters, then another voice. "Oh, Gord, you're wicked." I recognized it as that of Rona somebody, Gord's girlfriend.

I don't think Nancy heard. If she had, she probably would have gone over and torn off his lips.

The games were silly kids' games but a lot of fun. Neither of them relied on vision to play — in fact the second one was identifying objects by touch. I could have easily won, but I didn't want to draw attention to myself, so I purposely missed a few. Naturally, Gord Hadley had a comment to make about that, but he was quickly shut up by Johnny Sterling.

After the games there was more dancing, which I managed to avoid by getting into a deep conversation with a guy from the chess club who had seen me playing Jimmy Chang the other day. Then about eleven o'clock Greer cleared the dance floor and had a couple of guys set up a long table for the supper. Fortunately the food was not served buffet style, which is difficult for me. Rather it was served by a couple of women from the catering service that Greer's parents had hired to do the meal. A girl I didn't know sat on my left and Gord's Rona was on my right. The strange girl introduced herself as Milly something, then, to my astonishment, quietly explained where the food was on the plate, so I got through the main course without a problem. The trouble came with the ginger ale, which was served with dessert.

The birthday cake was brought in, alight with candles, and Greer did the usual making a wish and blowing them out. Then she cut the cake and one of the maids passed the pieces around. At the same time the other maid was filling the champagne glasses. I hate those top-heavy flutes. They're a menace to a sighted person, let alone someone who can't see. The slightest touch causes them to topple over. I was, therefore, extra careful to position the glass well away from the edge of the table and to the left of my plate where I could get to it without an accident.

When everyone had been served Johnny stood up and made a long funny speech that had everyone roaring with laughter.

"Now if everyone will take their glass in their hand," Johnny finished, "we'll all toast the birthday girl." There was a shuffle of feet and the sound of chairs being pushed back. Then silence while everyone waited for Johnny to continue. I reached for my glass where I had so carefully positioned it, and to my horror my arm hit another glass sitting on the edge of the table to my right. A moment later there was a shriek and Rona's shrill voice filled the room.

"You stupid, clumsy oaf! You've spilled it all over my new suede skirt! It'll never come out!"

I had no idea how the glass got there. One of the maids must have put down an extra. I started to apologize, but Rona was up and out of the room, still muttering about her ruined skirt before I could get the words out. Everyone was looking at me; I could feel it. You could cut the tension in the room with a dull butter knife. I wanted to crawl under the table and never come out. I'd made a fool of myself and everyone was feeling embarrassed and uncomfortable. Nancy was no doubt wishing she'd never invited me. God knows what Greer was thinking! The silence hung on for what felt like a couple of hours, then, from directly across the table came Gord's sneering voice. "Nice going, Hal. What do you do for an encore?"

"That's enough, Gord." Johnny's voice was sharp and not too friendly. "Let's get on with the toast." He started to speak and I reached more carefully for my glass. It wasn't there. The glass I'd knocked over must have been my own. But I knew I'd put it at least a foot from the edge of the table and on the left of my plate. There was only one explanation. Someone had moved it when everyone's attention was on Johnny. And who else but Gord Hadley?

When the meal was finally over and Nancy had gone to the ladies' room I began searching for Gord. I circled the room until I heard his loud voice telling someone about his brilliant football career. I stepped over to where I figured he would be standing and said, "Okay, Hadley, I've had it with you. If you don't stop hassling me I'm going to . . ."

"Oh, it's you, Drucker. What the hell's your problem?"

"You deliberately moved that glass so I'd knock it over, didn't you?" I was so angry that I could feel I was about to lose it.

"I don't know what you're talking about. I didn't touch your glass. Now get lost."

I stepped closer and made a lunge at him, but he must have anticipated my move. He stepped aside and I stumbled forward and crashed into the wall. The girl he'd been talking to started to giggle. Gord's braying laugh joined in. I didn't know if anyone else had seen my clumsy attempt, but I didn't stay around to find out. My anger had disappeared and total humiliation had taken its place. I turned and walked away.

I didn't bother to look for Nancy. Instead I stopped the first person I ran into and asked him where I could find a phone. He offered to make the call for me in such an overly solicitous manner that I knew he was still feeling uncomfortable about the ginger ale incident. I told him I'd prefer to make it myself, so he took me upstairs and showed me where the phone was. I asked him to tell Nancy I'd left, then called a cab and waited in the front hall, hoping no one would be leaving early and find me there. But it didn't work out that way.

"Where the heck do you think you're going, Hal Drucker?" Nancy's voice proceeded her down the hall to where I was standing.

"Home," I muttered. "I called a cab."

"Well, isn't that just peachy keen! You're just going to leave without even having the courtesy to thank your hostess, let alone let your date know. That's real class, that is."

"I figured you'd be glad to be rid of me," I answered, matching her anger. "Greer, too. I practically ruined her party and humiliated you in the bargain."

"What are you raving about? You didn't ruin anything. Everyone's forgotten all about you knocking over a glass. It could happen to anyone. Besides, Rona loves to overdramatize the slightest thing, and everyone knows it."

"Nancy, you're a good friend, but you're blowing smoke rings. I don't fit in. I'm different. I'm handicapped. Don't you understand? The social scene is not for me, so for pete's sake stop pushing me!"

At that moment a horn honked outside and I threw the door open and ran for it. Ten minutes later I was home and in my room, safe from the uncomfortable pity of my so-called peers.

Nine

When I woke up Sunday morning I lay in bed thinking for the better part of an hour. I could hear the family in the kitchen laughing and talking, but I wasn't ready to face anyone just yet. I knew they would want to know all about the party, and I wasn't looking forward to talking about it. Not yet — not until I'd got some things straight in my mind.

I had to admit to myself that I'd treated Nancy pretty badly. I should have told her I was leaving. The same with Greer. But that didn't change the fact I had proved to myself and everyone else I just couldn't hack the social scene. I vowed then and there I would never let myself get caught in a situation like last night ever again. I didn't need that kind of hassle. I would bury myself in my schoolwork and maybe in the chess club. I was smart; I knew that. I could graduate at the top of my class if I put my mind to it. That would assure me of getting into a good university, even if I was blind.

Then there was Gord Hadley. I had no idea why he was determined to bait me, but I did know I was going to find a way to get back at him. That dirty trick with the wineglass was the last straw.

I was just starting to visualize what I might do to Gord when there was a knock on the door and Pete called out, "Hey, Hal, aren't you going to come to breakfast? Mom's got French toast and back bacon all ready to eat."

He sounded more like his old self, I thought, as I felt my watch for the time. Maybe he was over his anger. I certainly hoped so. Life in the big bad outside world was rotten enough without having to put up with anger and resentment at home. "I'll be ready in a minute," I called back, climbing out of bed. "Come on in."

The door opened and Pete walked over to the chair by the desk and sat down.

"You were home early last night," he remarked with a question in his voice.

"Yeah." I stripped off my pajama bottoms and dashed into my bathroom. The last thing I wanted was a grilling of what had happened at Greer's. I had a quick shower, brushed my teeth and threw on a pair of jeans and a sweatshirt that were hanging on the peg behind the door. I figured Pete would be gone when I came out. He wasn't.

"I heard you come home. I also saw the cab leave. What happened, Hal?"

"You don't want to know," I answered. "Come on, let's go. I'm starving."

"You might as well tell me. I'll find out from Nancy anyway"

"Look, I made a fool of myself, humiliated Nancy and spoiled Greer's party. Satisfied?"

"No. You still haven't told me what happened."

I sighed. "Okay. I guess you won't shut up until I do." I dropped onto the bed and gave him a condensed version of the whole fiasco. I tried to explain how angry and embarrassed I was. "So I tried to punch out Gord Hadley, made a greater fool of myself and then took off," I finished.

"But what about Nancy? Did you just leave her there?"

"Of course. She was having a good time — at least she was until I screwed up. Why should she leave just because I couldn't take it any longer?"

"Oh, Hal," Pete sighed. "Nobody pays any attention to a spilled drink. It happens all the time — even to people with twenty-twenty vision," he added with a smile in his voice. "And nobody would blame you for taking a punch at Gord, even if you did miss. You're too sensitive."

"Easy for you to say," I answered more sharply than I intended. "Nobody pities you."

"And they won't pity you, either, if you let them get to know you. People forget about a handicap very quickly, believe me. Let me tell you about this guy who came to work at the office where I had a job last summer. He was a paraplegic and used a wheelchair. At first everyone was a little uncomfortable with him, mostly because we didn't know what to expect of him. Then we got to know him and became so accustomed to him that we would to do stupid, thoughtless things like ask him if he wanted to take the stairs or the elevator when we left the cafeteria to go back to our office. We totally forgot he was in a wheelchair."

"That's hard to believe," I answered.

"It's true, though. Sure, people feel bad for you. You're blind. It makes things tough. But that doesn't mean they pity you or think you're some sort of freak. Give them a chance."

I got up from the bed and walked over to the door. "Thanks for the lecture, little brother, but you really don't understand. You never will. Nobody will." I opened the door and walked down to the kitchen.

Nancy called while I was mopping up the last bit of syrup with the crust of my French toast. Pete answered the phone and I whispered to him to tell her I wasn't there.

"He's right here, Nancy," he said instead. "Just a sec and I'll take the phone over to him." He came around the table and shoved the phone in my hand, then left the room. Mom muttered something to Dad about getting ready for work and they followed Pete out the door.

I won't bore you with a detailed description of our conversation. It was pretty much a replay of the one we had at Greer's house the night before except for the finale.

"A bunch of us started a club last semester, Hal.

It's called SAFE, Students Advocating a Fit Environment, and we'd like you to join. You're really good at writing; you could help us with slogans and stuff like that. We meet at noon every Sunday for brunch and to work on our campaign. Today it's at Greer's. It's pretty short notice, but if you could be ready in half an hour I'll pick you up and drive you over."

Just like that! No Do you want to come? Just the bland assumption that I'd naturally accept. After all, what could a poor blind guy have to do on a Sunday anyway?

"I'm sorry," I answered, trying to control my anger. "But I have something planned. Thanks for the invitation. Maybe some other time." Then before she could try changing my mind I said, "See you in school tomorrow," and hung up the phone.

Of course I didn't have anything planned. I could go to church with Dad and Pete, but the idea of the crowds of people and Mom and Dad's friends trying to act natural around me was not my idea of a fun Sunday. I could do something with Pete after church, I supposed, but he had his own friends and I was determined not to horn in on his plans. The one thing I wasn't going to do, though, was go back to the scene of the most humiliating night of my life. Nancy should have known better than to even suggest it.

So I went downstairs and worked on a paper for Mrs. Oliver's English class. It was comparing two poems about dying: a Browning and a Tennyson. The theme fitted my mood exactly.

* * *

The next morning I left for school fifteen minutes early. I wanted to be gone before Nancy came by. I know it was a cowardly thing to do, but I wasn't ready for another lecture on how I shouldn't let my handicap get in the way of leading a peachy-keen life. Pete was still in the shower when I left, so I walked to school alone. It was a little scary knowing there was no one behind me if I got into trouble, but I made it just fine. My confidence in my ability to take care of myself was growing stronger every day. Pretty soon I wouldn't need anyone.

The custodian opens the school early on cold days so the kids who come early don't have to hang around outside. I went directly to homeroom and checked the batteries on my tape recorder. They were getting pretty weak, so I changed them, then settled down to wait for the rest of the kids to show up. Ten minutes later Mr. McGregor was calling the class to order.

"We're going to try something a little different for our midterm exam," he announced after he'd taken the roll and read the announcements. "Instead of writing a paper or taking an exam, we're going to have a series of debates. The class will be broken into pairs, and I will assign a different topic to each pair. You will all research your particular topic, then be prepared to present whichever view you are given — either the affirmative or the negative." He picked up the class list and started reading out names, coupling the students alphabetically.

"Drucker and Hadley," he read a moment later. For a moment I was furious. Me, paired with the bane of my existence. Then I began to smile as it suddenly hit me. I'd been handed the perfect opportunity to get back at Gord Hadley for all the crud he'd been giving me. I'd show him up so badly in the debate he'd be the laughingstock of the whole school.

Our topic was "Resolved that Harry Truman acted wisely in ordering the use of the atomic bomb against Japan," and I was given the negative. We had two weeks to research our assignment, then on Monday of the third week we would start the debates. Two pairs would present their arguments each day.

For the next two weeks I did nothing but study and play chess and computer games. I continued to get top marks in math and my essay on the "dying" poems rated an A+, the only one in the class. Mrs. Oliver even read it aloud. I played chess every Tuesday at the club with Jimmy Chang and most weekends with Hose. Every evening after I'd done my homework I sat at Gabby and played one of the half-dozen games I'd bought with Christmas money from my aunt. As predicted I was invited to be on the school chess team and take part in the inter-city tournament in March.

I didn't talk to either Nancy or Greer at school other than to say hi. Nancy apparently got my message and didn't bug me any more about dating. Greer, that first Monday after her party, stopped me and tried to apologize for Gord and his girlfriend, but I brushed it off with a shrug and tried not to look as uncomfortable as I felt.

It wasn't till the Friday before our debates started that Nancy sought out Hose and me at our table in the far corner of the cafeteria. She put her tray on the table across from me and sat down beside Hose as if it were the most ordinary thing in the world.

"I just heard you made the chess team, Hal. Congratulations," she said, banging her plate and glass on the table and dropping her tray to the floor. "You're getting to be quite a celebrity."

"It's just the chess team. No big deal. It's not like I made first-string quarterback."

"It is so a big deal," Hose retorted. "Everybody knows you're the best in the school. Even better than Jimmy Chang."

"I also hear you're doing very well in your classes. Aceing exams and having your papers read aloud. Very impressive."

Somehow she didn't sound at all impressed. I wondered what she was up to. Two bites of my burger and a gulp of milk later I found out.

"But then I guess you have more time than the rest of us to study, don't you? I mean, since you don't take in any of the school functions or work on any of the school projects. Right?"

"I don't have time for fooling around, Nancy. I need to get the highest marks I can if I expect to go to a decent university." I wondered if Pete had told her about all the time I spent with the mindless computer games, and decided he probably had.

He'd certainly made it plain enough to me what he thought of my solitary pastime.

"Sure, Hal. Well, if you think you can tear yourself away from your books next Saturday, why don't you come to the Valentine dance? No, wait, I'm not asking you to take me," she hurried on as I started to protest. "I already have a date. But lots of kids are going stag. You might have fun."

For the weirdest reason I suddenly felt jealous. Somebody else was taking Nancy to the dance. Not that I would have asked her myself, of course, but the idea of someone else dating her really got to me.

"Hey, that's a great idea, Hal," Hose said enthusiastically. "I sure would like to go, but I don't want to go alone. We could go stag."

"I'll think about it," I muttered, sounding childishly sullen even to my own ears.

"Do that." She got up and without saying goodbye walked away.

"So how about it, Hal?" Hose asked.

I thought for a minute. I could go with Hose and stand around the sidelines. It would show Nancy she was wrong about me being anti-social — afraid to take part in school activities. And with Hose there I wouldn't have to do anything that would be embarrassing, like trying to dance. I'd just have to stay a short time, then when I was sure Nancy saw me I'd split.

Besides, I could always beg off at the last moment, I reasoned. If it didn't seem like such a good idea when the time actually came to go to the dance I'd just tell Hose I couldn't make it. It was a whole week away. A lot could happen in that time.

"Sure. Why not?" I answered with a shrug. "It might be good for a laugh."

Ten

I had been working on my arguments for the debate ever since we had been given our topics. I felt pretty confident I could easily win, but I wanted to do more than just defeat Gord Hadley. I wanted to pulverize him. So I spent most of that weekend figuring out every possible argument for the affirmative, Gord's position, and destroying it. By the time Monday morning came, I was ready. However, when Mr. McGregor posted the order of the debates on the board at the beginning of class I found that Gord and I weren't up until Friday, the final day.

I had done a lot of formal debating at the school for the blind in my last two years there, and I was pretty familiar with all the rules and the tricks. What I saw in that history class was *not* what I was used to. First, the debate wasn't really a debate at all. One kid gave his side of the issue and his opponent gave the other side. Neither paid any attention to what his partner had said. In other words, there was no such thing as rebuttal. The more I heard as the days went by, the more confident I was that when our time came I would make Gord Hadley look like a total klutz.

When Friday morning finally came around I was feeling pretty good about myself. I'd beaten Jimmy Chang two games in a row the previous Tuesday and Marigold told me, in front of the whole club, that she'd never seen anyone my age play as well. Jimmy was nice about losing, congratulating me and saying how fortunate it was that I'd come to Churchill and joined the club. It was kind of funny, though; no one else said anything to me about the win. Hose made sure everyone in the caf knew about it the next day, but it wasn't like that time in the gym when he announced my first win over Jimmy. Kids didn't come over and congratulate me. In fact, no one said much of anything. I felt hurt at first, then I told myself it didn't matter what the kids did or didn't do. The only thing that counted in the long run was coming out on top.

Not only had I proved myself to be the best chess player in the school, but I'd been asked to be on Teen Tourney, a local quiz show kind of like "Jeopardy!" As a result of these two achievements, my self-confidence was at an all-time high. So when Mr. McGregor called on us to present our arguments first thing Friday morning I was ready to make Gord Hadley sorry he'd ever been born.

We had each been given ten minutes to talk. Gord spoke first, and as I'd anticipated, he laid on the old argument about the end justifying the means. By ordering the dropping of the atom bomb, Truman put an end to a war that was taking thousands of lives. That was his big point. His only point, I might add. He stumbled around for about five minutes saying the same thing over and over again, then sat down.

I took my full ten minutes, the first five presenting my arguments and the last five tearing Gord's argument to bits. It was a piece of cake. By the time I'd finished I'd made the sleaze sound like he'd never had an original thought in his entire life — which may well have been the case. I guess I got a little personal a couple of times, but it was not more than he deserved.

Mr. McGregor heaped on the praise for the way I'd organized my material and presented it. Then he put the icing on the cake by criticizing Gord for his total lack of preparation — comparing his presentation to mine in very unfavorable terms.

When the last couple were finished, Mr. McGregor thanked us all for our efforts and said he would post our grades inside the classroom door at noon. The bell rang and everyone scrambled to get to their next class. As I was pushing myself through the crowd I bumped into Greer Jordon. I knew it was her before she even spoke. The rose perfume.

"Oh, sorry, Hal," she muttered.

"No, it was my fault," I replied. Then, feeling confident over the way I'd handled myself in class, I started to walk along beside her. "How did you like the debate?" I asked hopefully. But if I'd expected her to fall all over me for the way I'd demolished Hadley, I had a big surprise coming.

"I don't like that sort of thing — you know, where one person wins at the expense of another person. I'd rather the teachers just stuck to tests and reports." Then before I could reply she broke away and hurried ahead of me down the hall.

I was a little late getting out of science lab, so when I went to find out what kind of mark McGregor had given me I discovered a three-deep crowd around the door. They were all talking at once, either complaining or exulting over the mark they got. I couldn't make out much until Gord Hadley's irate voice cut through the chatter.

"Geez, would you look at that? The creep gave me an F! That really screws up my average."

I couldn't keep the grin off my face as I called out, "Could someone read me my grade?"

No one answered for a moment. Then a voice I didn't recognize said, "You got an A, of course. What did you expect, Einstein?"

There were a few muffled giggles, then the voice continued. "Tough luck, Gord."

"Yeah, too bad." "You deserved better" and other sundry remarks came from the crowd around me. No one said anything about my grade.

I couldn't believe it. Everyone was feeling sorry for Gord Hadley — the school loudmouth and insensitive boor — and treating me like I had a social disease. I turned and rushed down the hall to the cafeteria before I heard anything more.

Hose was already at our usual table when I got

there. He stopped eating and asked me what I wanted, reeling off the day's menu. I ordered a ham sandwich and milk and gave him my money. When he returned with my tray I told him what had happened in the debate and how the kids had acted over Gord's and my grades. I expected the usual non-stop monologue filled with praise and a lot of non sequiturs that was Hose's method of communication. But he surprised me.

"Yeah, I heard about the debate," Hose answered cautiously. "We don't have history till third period, you know, and by then the word had got out that you wiped the floor with Gord Hadley."

"So why is everyone acting like I committed a particularly unsavory offense?"

"I guess the kids thought you were too rough on Gord. You're really smart, Hal, and Gord has trouble writing his name. Nobody likes Gord a helluva lot, but . . . well, there's a feeling that you took advantage of him."

"My God, Hose!" I bellowed, not caring who heard me. "After all the lousy things he did to me, I'm being criticized for trying to get my own back?"

"Don't yell at me, Hal. I tried to defend you." I heard him push his chair back and pick up his tray. "Look, I gotta go. McGregor said he'd have our grades for us after lunch. I want to see if I got a B. I really need it, but McGregor marks hard. He practically never gives out an A." This last remark sounded almost accusatory.

Well, to hell with you, my friend, I thought as I

bit viciously into my sandwich. Go ahead and follow the pack. Who needs you? I finished my lunch alone and wandered off to my next class long before the afternoon bell sounded. For the first time since that initial week at Churchill I was wishing I was back at the school for the blind. It wasn't the greatest place in the world, but at least no one made a pariah out of you for being smart.

* * *

I guess I underestimated Hose's loyalty, however. The next day he phoned early in the afternoon to see what time I wanted him to pick me up that evening. To be honest, I'd forgotten all about the Valentine dance, what with the debate and its mixed consequences. I'd been brooding all morning, running the scene at the grade posting and Hose's behavior in the caf over and over in my mind, so when I heard his voice my first reaction was to tell him to go to hell.

I thought better of it, though, as I realized I wanted to go to the dance and I needed him to go with me. I was determined to show everyone how little I cared for their opinion of me — particularly Nancy. She'd no doubt heard about my horrible treatment of poor little defenseless Gord Hadley and like everyone else was repulsed by it.

I swallowed my anger and made my voice as pleasant as I could.

"What time does it start?"

"Seven-thirty, but no one but the Grade 9s get there until after eight."

"So what about eight-thirty?" I wanted to be sure

Nancy and the rest of my so-called friends would be there before I arrived.

"Fine. See you then." I waited for him to hang up. "Ah, Hal," he said a moment later, "I really am glad we're going together. I hate to go to these things alone."

"Why?" I asked in surprise. Hose seemed so sure of himself — the supreme extrovert.

"I'm pretty shy, Hal. I'd like to ask a girl — Betsy Bonner, to be exact — but I can't get up the nerve. I know she's not going with anyone and I'm hoping to maybe have a few dances with her."

I couldn't help laughing. Poor Hose. If he couldn't get up the nerve to ask her for a date, how was he going to ask her to dance? Well, that was his problem. I wouldn't be sticking around long enough to find out how it came out anyway.

"Okay, see you at eight-thirty." I hung up and I went to find Pete to ask him what I should wear.

I hadn't talked to my brother other than table chatter since Thursday night. I'd avoided him on Friday, knowing that he'd no doubt heard about the debate and not wanting to get a lecture on how I should behave. I found him downstairs, working at the computer.

"Oh, hi, Hal," he said quickly. "I'm sorry. I'll stop right now."

"No, I don't want Gabby," I hastened to assure him. "Besides, even if I did, this is your Saturday to have it."

"Yeah, sure." His voice was filled with irony. "So what did you want?"

I ignored the tone and answered the question. Pete still acted as though the computer was mine alone and he was taking liberties if he used it. Nothing I said seemed to change his mind.

"What are you wearing to the dance tonight? You *are* going, aren't you?"

"Yeah, I'm going. Why?"

"I just wanted to know what I should wear. I don't want to look out of place."

"I didn't know you were planning to go, Hal." He sounded both pleased and anxious. "Are you taking anyone?"

"No. Hose and I are going stag. Are you?"

"Well, yes." He hesitated, then murmured, "I'm taking Nancy."

"Nancy!" I repeated, taken aback. "I didn't think you liked her," I added, reminding him of his description of her. "You seemed to think she was pretty much of a dog."

"She's no Greer Jordon," he answered, "but she'd a real nice kid. Too bad you couldn't see that for yourself."

"You seem to forget I can't see anything," I snapped. I was immediately sorry for the cheap shot, but I couldn't make myself apologize. For some stupid reason I was too angry that he was dating Nancy. Before he could say anything more I left the room and phoned Hose back to tell him I wouldn't be going to the dance after all.

Eleven

Hose didn't say much when I told him I couldn't go with him. He didn't even ask why I had changed my mind. I figured he'd find someone else to team up with and forgot all about it as my mind went back to Pete and Nancy.

I couldn't understand why I was so upset that they were going to the dance together. I had no romantic interest in Nancy, that was for sure. She was a real nice girl, but I couldn't get my mind off Greer Jordon. I suppose it was just a case of blind envy — forgive the pun. The idea of Pete and Nancy off having a good time together while I tried to beat the computer playing chess really got to me.

I was in bed before Pete got in late that night and I managed to avoid him the next day. I didn't want to hear about the great time he'd had or have to explain why I had canceled out at the last minute. However, that evening when I was leaving my room, where I'd been holed up all day, to go down for dinner I heard Mom and Dad talking to Pete about me.

"He's turning into such a lone wolf," Mom said. "I'm getting worried."

"It's what he wants, I guess," Pete answered.

"No one *wants* to be a loner, Pete. He's having a bad time adjusting and you should be helping him." Dad sounded angry.

"He doesn't want my help," Pete contradicted him. "He's turning everyone against him, even Hose Como, who gets along with everybody. He was supposed to go to the dance last night with Hose, then at the last minute he phoned and canceled. No explanation. I saw Hose at the roller rink this afternoon and he was really ticked off."

"I'm sure he had a very good reason for not going, son," Mom contended. "It can't be easy for him to suddenly have to cope in a sighted world after having been sheltered for so many years at the school. He must feel very out of place and uncomfortable."

"Your mother is right, Peter. I want you to make a greater effort to help him adjust. It's the least you can do!"

I didn't want to hear any more of the forum on what to do with poor Hal, so I slipped back into my room. I started to ease the door shut, but before I got it closed, Pete's voice, choked with tears, came softly down the hall. "I'm sorry. I'll try to help him. I don't know what I can do to get him to mix with other kids but I'll try."

"Well, see that you do. It's your . . ." I didn't wait to hear any more. Closing the door, I went over and threw myself down on the bed. I wanted to tell Pete I was sorry for causing him so much trouble, but what could I say? I *was* a lone wolf and I was perfectly content to be one. That way I couldn't get hurt. But it wasn't fair that Pete should have to take the flak for it. Why couldn't Dad leave him alone? And why didn't Pete fight back?

* * *

On Monday I had Mom make me a lunch so I wouldn't have to go through the lineup. I finished my science experiment early, so when I got to the caf at eleven-forty-five it was nearly deserted. I found a small table at the back and started eating my sandwich, hoping I'd be through and out of there before Hose came in. If he really was ticked off, like Pete said, he'd probably ignore me and sit with some of his other friends. I guess I wouldn't blame him, either, but I wasn't about to set myself up to be put down by him. I hurried through my lunch and was tossing my garbage into the trash basket when I heard footsteps approaching, then Hose's voice.

"Hey, where are you going? Aren't you gonna have lunch?"

"Oh, hi," I answered, flustered. "I've already eaten." I grabbed up my book bag and, feeling like the jerk of the century, stumbled my way through the crowds and out of the room.

* * *

I stuck to the same routine for the rest of the week,

brown-bagging it alone in the cafeteria and leaving as soon as I had finished. I would have avoided the caf entirely if I could have, but it was against the rules to eat anywhere else in the school. Hose never came over to my table again; I guess he'd about had it with me, and I didn't blame him. I missed him, though. He was in homeroom with me and in chess club, but we didn't speak. In fact, I spoke to hardly anyone that week or the following week.

As soon as school was out I would rush home and head downstairs to play chess with the computer until dinnertime. It was the best practice I could get, better than playing with a live opponent. The inter-city match was coming up in just two weeks and I needed all the practice I could get. In the evenings when Pete wasn't using the computer or I had finished my homework on it I played another couple of matches. By the end of that first week I was actually beating it every ten or so games. It was just like playing with a real person except the computer was smarter than most amateur chess players. It told me every move it made and apologized when it checkmated me. It was kind of a lonely existence, but I told myself I didn't mind. I needed all my time to study and practice.

I waited all week to see what, if anything, Pete would do about Dad's injunction to get me into the social swim. I certainly had no intention of accepting an invitation to go anywhere with him and his gang, and I'd tell him so the moment he suggested it. I'd vowed when I first came home that I wouldn't be a drag on him, and I meant to stick to it. Every day I expected him to make some casual offer to take me somewhere with him and every day I prepared a new excuse as to why I couldn't go. But the whole week went by without so much as a suggestion to have a burger together after school. Then late Saturday afternoon the bomb dropped.

I was sitting up in my room going over some taped notes when Pete knocked on my door and walked in.

"Hey, Hal, come on downstairs. A bunch of kids dropped in, and we're going to have a party."

I whirled around in my chair.

"A party? At this time of day?" I checked my watch. "It's only five-thirty."

"I know. It's a supper party. Dad's making chili and garlic bread for us." He walked over to the desk where I was sitting and gave me a shove. "So get the lead out, eh?"

"I can't, Pete. I have to study."

"Come on, man. It's Saturday night. You can study tomorrow. Now move it. I won't take no for an answer."

I knew I'd have to go. For Pete's sake. If I didn't, Dad would be on his case for not making me join in. I figured I could go for supper, then make some excuse to leave early. That way Pete would do his duty and I wouldn't be a drag on him.

"Okay, give me a minute to wash up and change my shirt and I'll be down." I got up and went into my bathroom, grabbing a clean shirt on the way.

When I came out a few minutes later Pete was still in the room.

"It's okay," I said a little testily as I reached for my hairbrush. "I said I'd come down and I will. You don't have to stick around to personally escort me."

"No sweat," he answered nonchalantly and continued to stand in the doorway. I slapped my brush down on the dresser and walked toward him.

"Okay, let's go and get this over with."

There seemed to be about twenty kids all gathered around the computer when Pete and I arrived downstairs. When they saw us they demanded we show them how Gabby works.

"Let Hal show you," Pete suggested. "He's the expert."

There was nothing for me to do but comply, so, feeling a little like a side-show act, I turned on the computer. My chess disk was still in it, so I gave them a demonstration of how the program played with me, its mechanical voice telling me every move it made. Everyone wanted to try it, of course, and most of the kids were still gathered around when Dad arrived with the food.

Maybe it was because I was on my own home turf, but I found, after my initial anxiety about walking into that crowded room and suddenly being the center of attention, that I was having a pretty good time. I didn't know Pete's gang very well; a lot of them were a year behind me, but they couldn't have been more friendly. Or laid-back about my blindness.

They all helped themselves to the food, as I did. I didn't need assistance getting my chili and stuff or finding a convenient place to eat. After all, I was in my own home, not the crowded caf. It felt good. I sat with a couple of guys I hadn't met before who started talking about our local baseball team's chances of taking the triple A pennant this year. They made sure I was included in the conversation, assuming I was a baseball fan like everyone else at Churchill High.

Everyone was talking at top pitch. Then there occurred one of those strange silences that sometimes happen when everyone seems to stop talking at the same time. Everyone except one person.

"He seems to be having a good time, Pete. The kids are —" Nancy Adams stopped in midsentence.

The silence was broken as everyone began to babble at once. I forced myself to swallow the spoonful of chili I'd taken in my mouth just before Nancy spoke. It tasted like mud. I picked up my plate, took it over to the table and left the room.

Twelve

*T*he whole thing had been a setup. Pete and Nancy had cooked the party up between them to get Pete off the hook with our parents. Obviously Nancy didn't want me to know she was there in case I caught on to their scheme. I could just imagine Pete telling his friends, Look, you guys, my brother Hal hasn't got any social life and my dad is on my case to help him. So I'm throwing this party. I want you all to come and make sure he has a good time. Make him feel wanted.

I rolled over on my stomach and punched the pillow. I hadn't cried since I was ten years old, but I was sure close to tears then. I was furious with Pete, with Nancy, with Dad, with everybody who had taken part in this charade. Why couldn't they just leave me alone? I didn't *need* anybody. Why couldn't they get that through their heads?

A few minutes after I'd closed the door to my room Pete showed up. He didn't even bother to knock.

"Hey, Hal. What's the matter? Why did you leave?"

"You have to ask?" I mumbled through the pillow.

"Yeah, I have to ask. You seemed to be having a great time, then just like that you take off. Everyone's wondering what got into you."

"Look, Pete, don't do me any more favors, okay? And you can tell your friend Nancy Adams that next time she wants to take advantage of my blindness by not letting me know she's in the room, she should keep her stupid mouth shut."

"Oh, that. I can explain, Hal. See, Nancy and I —"

"Pete," I interrupted, rolling over and sitting up, "I don't care what you and Nancy did or thought or planned. Just don't do it anymore. Now will you please shut the door as you go out." I grabbed the earphones off my night table, turned the volume up on my tape recorder and lay back on the bed.

* * *

Naturally Mom and Dad were upset about the whole thing. They came into my room later in the evening and tried to find out what had happened.

"Nothing happened," I lied. "It was a good party; it was nice of Pete to include me. But I got kind of bored after a while, so I left and came up here to listen to some tapes." I hoped that would satisfy them and at the same time get Pete off the hook. Furious as I was at him, I didn't want him to get into any more trouble with the folks over me.

They didn't comment, but Mom's quiet little

sigh said it all. Poor Hal. He's such a worry. Whatever are we going to do about him?

Pete tried a couple more times to talk to me about the party, but I cut him off. Finally he got the message and stopped bugging me. He remained polite and ever helpful, but the close feeling we'd always had was no longer there.

The next week was a repeat of the first: brown-bagging it alone at lunch; walking to and from school alone; studying and playing chess with Gabby. I got a talking book out of the library on famous chess moves and spent a lot of time studying and memorizing it. The rest of the time I worked on my assignments. It paid off, too. I aced a geometry test, brought my French mark up to an A and had my paper on Emerson read in class.

These things, however, didn't make me the most popular kid on the block. Oh, sure, the teachers were delighted with me. I was their star pupil. But the kids seemed to resent it whenever I was singled out for an honor. Especially Gord Hadley. He'd started calling me Einstein, in his sneering tone, and it had caught on.

I didn't care, though. What did it matter to me what a bunch of pea-brains with nothing on their minds but sex and baseball thought of me? I needed good grades far more than I needed to be Mr. Popularity.

The week passed by slowly until finally it was Saturday, the first day of the chess tournament.

The tournament was held downtown in the Convention Center. Dad drove me and came into the building to help me find the right room. It turned out to be in the basement, a huge area filled with small tables, two chairs at each. We were told when we went up to register me that there were nine high schools competing, each with a team of four players. Each team member would play a game with a team member from two other schools, thus assuring that every school played every other school once. The maximum number of games a school could win would therefore be eight. The two top teams would play off the next day, three members from each team playing one game each.

I signed in and was given a table number and the names of the two people I would be playing. Dad read them out to me and helped me find my table.

"There's quite a crowd here already, Hal," he told me. "The stands are nearly full and it's still fifteen minutes before the matches begin."

"Are the rest of the players all here?" I asked.

"About half, I'd say. Well, if you're okay I'll leave you and go up into the stands with the rest of the spectators."

"Sure, I'm fine, but you don't have to stick around. I'll get a ride home with someone."

"Wouldn't miss it for anything. Too bad your mom can't be here, but she's specialing on a serious case and couldn't take the time off."

He didn't mention why Pete didn't come and I didn't ask.

When he left I sat down at the table and waited for the games to begin. I was wondering if any of my teammates had arrived when someone came over to my table and sat down.

"Hi, Hal. It's Jimmy. How are you feeling?"

"A little nervous," I admitted. "I suppose you're used to this, eh?"

"You're *never* used to it," he answered. "Who did you draw to play?"

"I didn't draw anyone. The guy at the desk just gave me two names: Ron Sykes and Boris Kamarov."

Jimmy laughed. "I didn't mean you *personally* drew the names. A computer does that." He paused then went on. "Ron is a so-so player; you shouldn't have any trouble beating him. Boris is a different story. No one knows how good he is, but his being Russian makes me nervous. I think they're all born with special chess genes."

"Oh, God!" I muttered. "Why me?"

"Don't worry. He may be a total flop, and you're darn good yourself, Hal."

"What about the rest of our team? How did you all make out?"

"Lucky. The rest of us have pretty easy matches except for Keith. We found out his first opponent is Cathy Wicks. She's on the Bishop Grady team and, next to Don Devereau, the person to beat."

"Hal Drucker?" someone said beside me.

"Yes, that's me," I answered.

"Ron Sykes."

Jimmy pushed his chair back and stood up. "Guess I'd better get to my table. See you at break, Hal. Lotsa luck." He walked off and Ron sat down in the chair he'd vacated.

"You're the blind guy," he informed me.

I agreed that he'd got that right and waited for the usual question. He didn't disappoint me.

"How do you keep track of the pieces? Do I have to keep describing the board or do you feel them?"

I laughed. "None of the above. I keep the board in my head. All you have to do is move my pieces for me where I tell you to, and let me know what your moves are."

"Are you sure?" He sounded dubious.

"I'm sure. Haven't you ever heard of guys playing with their backs to the board? Same thing."

Before he could quiz me further, the loudspeaker came to life and announced play would begin in one minute.

It wasn't much of a contest. Ron was one of those aggressive players who think bold moves are smart moves. I had him on the twenty-first move. He searched to find a way out, but it was obvious to both of us he was finished.

"Your move," I said with a grin, delighted that I'd won my first match. It would make it a little easier to face the Boris Kamarov threat.

"Okay, I resign," he grumbled ungraciously.

I laughed. He stood, knocking his chair over, and leaned across the table. I could feel his breath on my face.

"God, you're a conceited bastard!" he spat out. "I'd heard about your puffed-up ego but I didn't believe it until now. I hope your next opponent wipes the floor with you." He stomped away and I was left sitting at the table alone.

Thirteen

*I*t was two-thirty when I finished my game with Ron. I sat at the table after he'd left and tried to digest his angry outburst. I didn't think I was being egotistical in enjoying my win. What did he expect me to do? Put on a sad face and apologize for beating him? And what about that remark about hearing I was a conceited bastard? I felt a momentary hurt surge though me, then I mentally shrugged it off. He's just a poor loser, I told myself. He very likely made up that whole story to get back at me for winning.

I was beginning to wonder whether I should stay at my table or go looking for my teammates when the loudspeaker sputtered into action.

"All players who have completed their games may retire to the adjoining room where refreshments have been set up. The next round of play will begin at three-thirty."

I picked up my cane and rose, trying to figure

out where the door to the adjoining room might be. As I stood there hesitating, a hand took my arm and a voice I didn't recognize spoke to me.

"Hi. I am Boris Kamarov. We play the next match, I believe." I turned to him and nodded, noting with dismay his almost comic Russian accent and remembering what Jimmy had said about Russians and their chess genes. He continued. "Would you like I show you where is the room with the refreshments?"

"Thanks," I answered and took his proffered arm.

"How did your first match proceed?" he asked as we threaded our way through the tables.

"I won," I answered, trying to sound modest. "How about you?"

"Yes, I, too, was fortunate enough to defeat my opponent. She was not a great challenge. You, however, are another carton of fish, I understand."

"Kettle of fish," I corrected him with a laugh. "I don't know about that. This is my first tournament."

We reached the door and went out into the next room where the smell of fresh coffee and warm pastries made me realize how hungry I was. I had been too nervous to eat any lunch, and breakfast had consisted of half a piece of toast and a glass of milk. Boris led me to a table and asked me what I wanted him to bring me.

While he was off getting coffee and a cinnamon roll someone came over to the table and sat down.

"I see you're consorting with the enemy. Is he trying to weaken your defenses before he takes you on?" the person asked, then laughed.

"Oh, it's you, Jimmy!" I exclaimed. "Do you know how our team did? Are they all finished?"

"Everyone is done," he answered. "Jenny and I won our matches, but Cathy Wicks beat Keith. That leaves us down one and you in the catbird seat."

"What do you mean?"

"It looks like Bishop Grady is going to take all their matches. We need to win the next four to end up with seven. So does Granville High. If you lose to Boris, Granville High could end up with seven to our up six."

At that moment Boris returned with the coffee and a plate of rolls, which he handed me. "I will leave you now to attend my teammates," he announced. "Enjoy your repast. I look forward to our forthcoming encounter with eager anticipation." I swear he clicked his heels together before he walked away.

"Is he for real?" I asked around a mouthful of warm roll.

"He's real, all right, and deadly. I hear he took his first game in nine moves."

The roll I was chewing so eagerly suddenly turned to Silly Putty in my mouth and I nearly choked trying to swallow it.

When the loudspeaker announced the start of the second round of play a few minutes later I was back at my table taking deep breaths and repeating to myself that I was going to win. Positive thinking and all that. Boris arrived at the last minute and, slapping me on the shoulder cried, "May the worst man lose, Hal!"

"I think you mean, 'May the best man win,' Boris," I corrected him.

"I prefer it my way." He laughed and took his seat. "You wish me to move your pieces for you?"

"Please," I answered. "Pawn to Queen Four." And the match began.

* * *

It was nearly five o'clock. The other matches had apparently finished and we were still at it. "Rook to King's Knight Four," Boris said. There was a gasp from the group around us watching the play. I reviewed the board in my head for a minute. He was obviously expecting me to move my Queen. I hesitated, then took a gamble that he wouldn't see what I was up to.

"Bishop to Queen Two."

"Are you sure?" Boris asked, surprised.

"I'm sure."

"Okay. King to Bishop Four."

I couldn't help the smile that spread across my face. He'd actually fallen into the trap. "Bishop to King Three. Check."

There was a moment of silence. Then from across the table Boris whispered, "I will be damned," and he tipped over his King.

A cheer went up from the group around the table and the remaining spectators in the stands.

"Way to go, Hal," Jimmy said from behind me.

"Your win, put us in the finals," Jenny announced. "We all won our games, but so did the others from Granville High."

Dad arrived just then and patted me on the

shoulder. "Well done, son. Are you ready to leave? You must be tired."

I suddenly realized I was exhausted. The tension of the past ninety minutes had completely drained me. I stood up and put my hand out. "Great game, Boris. Sorry we couldn't both be winners."

Boris took my hand and shook it vigorously. "I shall be here tomorrow to watch you perform, my friend. You are a formidable opponent. I shall expect to see you win."

At that moment I think I could have taken on Boris Spassky himself and beaten him in six moves.

* * *

The finals started at two on Sunday. Dad and I arrived a little before one-thirty since he had to catch a flight to Vancouver at two-fifteen. The room where we'd played the day before was nearly deserted.

"I can't tell you how sorry I am not to be able to stay for the match, Hal. Mom will be here to pick you up at five. She's leaving early today since she worked overtime last night. Will you be okay if I leave you here?"

"Of course," I replied a little testily. It looked like nobody from my family figured the match was important enough to bother attending. Okay, so Mom had to work and Dad had to catch a plane. But Pete could have come. I slumped dejectedly on the bottom row of the stands and waited for my teammates to arrive.

Ten minutes later the crowd started pouring in,

and Jimmy Chang appeared at my side. A moment later the other two joined us. Only three of us would play, making it a two-out-of-three contest. Jimmy, Jenny and I had been chosen since Keith had lost his game and volunteered to drop out.

The stands were full, Jimmy told me as we waited for the organizer to announce who would be playing whom and in which order. At five to two the PA squawked to life.

"First game: Halford Drucker versus Patrick Knowles."

"Good!" Jimmy exclaimed, taking my arm and leading me over to the table in the middle of the room. "I was hoping either you or I would get Pat. He's the weakest player on the Bishop Grady team. You should be able to beat him easily."

"I don't understand," I muttered. "Wouldn't it have been better if Jenny had got him?"

"No, of course not. We need to win two matches. Jenny is our weakest member and is the likeliest to lose, so better she lose to a strong player."

"Oh, I get it," I said as we approached the table and I felt for the chair. Then it hit me. "But what if I lose? It could happen, you know."

"You can't lose, Hal. We need your win if we're going to take the match."

Just what I needed to hear to make me feel like throwing up! I was beginning to wonder why I'd ever thought I'd want to play tournament chess. It was nothing but stress, mental agony and stomach cramps.

I was really nervous for the first couple of minutes, but four moves into the game I knew I could beat him. Pat Knowles played the same aggressive game that Ron Sykes played, and he made the same mistake Ron máde in thinking I was a pushover because I was blind. He made his first stupid play on his fifth move, his second on the ninth and I had him by the twelfth. The game was over in less than half an hour. Jimmy was at my side in a moment and leading me back to the stands.

One down; two to go.

"Game one — Churchill High," the loudspeaker reported. "Second game: Jennifer Gault versus Cathy Wicks."

Jenny jumped up and ran down to the floor. Jimmy groaned.

"I was hoping Jenny would get Devereau."

"So you wouldn't have to play him, is that right?"

"You've got it. He's my nemesis. I've only beaten him in a match once and we've played at least half a dozen. I think he's put a spell on me."

"Come on, Jimmy," I said with a laugh, feeling wonderful now that my game was over. "You can beat him if you just make up your mind to do it. Forget about all the other times he won. This is a brand-new ball game. Besides," I added hopefully, "maybe Jenny will beat Cathy Wicks."

"Maybe," he answered gloomily, "but don't bet the family farm on it. She's almost as good as Devereau."

A big board at the far end of the room charted the moves for the benefit of the spectators, Jimmy told me, but each move was announced on the loudspeaker as well, so I was able to follow the game easily. I would have been happier if I hadn't. Cathy took Jenny on the nineteenth move. That left the score one game each. Now it was up to Jimmy.

The loudspeaker announced that there would be a fifteen-minute break before the final match, so we all trooped into the adjoining room for a cup of coffee. Keith, Jenny and I, as well as all the kids who had come from the school to cheer us on, spent the whole recess period trying to psych Jimmy up. It was tough going. He really was convinced that Don Devereau had his number. When the bell rang summoning us back to the auditorium Jimmy was not exactly Mr. Cool.

"Final and deciding match: James Chang versus Donald Devereau," the PA announced.

"I'm a dead man!" Jimmy sighed and left our little group to take his place.

Jenny, Keith and I went up to the stand to watch, or in my case hear, the match. It was nerveracking. Jimmy was outstanding in the opening, then he seemed to lose steam during the middle game. In the endgame he came to life, and it was touch and go right up to the thirty-second move when he made a brilliant play and mated.

We'd won the tournament.

The spectators poured from the stands and surrounded the table, Jenny and Keith dragging me along between then.

"Terrific game, Jimmy!" someone cried. "Way to go, Chang," another person yelled. I felt the pressure of all those bodies surrounding me, and for a moment panic flooded over me. Then the crowd seemed to part and Jenny pushed me toward the front of the room.

"Come on. They want to take our picture," she told me. We reached the platform where the guy who called the plays was sitting and had our picture taken for the local paper. A couple of reporters asked us questions and we all answered at once.

Finally, it was over. The crowd began to disperse; the noise level dropped to a dull roar and I went over and sat down in the stands.

"Want a lift home, Hal?" Keith asked.

"Thanks, but my mom is picking me up."

"Okay. See you tonight at the victory party."

"Party?" I asked.

"Sure, there's always a party after the tournament. It's at the Holiday Inn."

"I don't care much for parties," I told him, thinking about my previous disastrous experiences with the social scene.

"Come on, Hal, you've got to be there. Team spirit and all that. Besides, don't you want to bask in the glory of our win? Look, I won't take no for an answer," he continued when I didn't say anything. "Jenny and I will pick you up at seven o'clock. Be ready."

And with that he walked away, leaving me sitting alone in the stands.

Fourteen

*T*he River Room at the Holiday Inn, where the party was being held, was packed when I arrived with Keith and Jenny. The crush of people at the door as we tried to get in brought on the familiar feeling of panic I have in a mob. Jenny must have noticed because she immediately took my hand and led me to a table at the far side of the room away from the crowd.

"Sit down and I'll get you something to drink. What do you want?"

"A soda would be great," I told her and sank gratefully into the nearest chair.

She hadn't been gone for more than a couple of minutes when someone pulled out a chair across from me and sat down.

"Hello. You're Hal Drucker, aren't you?" a male voice asked. He sounded like an older man, not one of the kids from school. I nodded and waited for him to go on.

"My name is Parker Cummings," he informed me, taking my hand from where it was resting on the table and shaking it. "I'm with the *Daily Courier* and I'd like to talk to you about the tournament."

"Sure," I answered. "What do you want to know?"

"Well, first," he said briskly, and I could hear him ruffling pages, "tell me how you learned to play chess so well."

"I learned from my father," I answered. "Then there was a teacher at the school for the blind who played with me nearly every evening. He was very good. But look, I thought you wanted to talk about the tournament."

"Oh, I do," he assured me. "You won all three of your games, didn't you? Did you feel they were a challenge?"

"Boris Kamarov is a great player. I had a lot of trouble beating him. I guess I just got lucky."

"What about the other two matches?"

"Ron Sykes and Pat Knowles weren't so difficult, although both played well. I guess maybe I had a bit of an advantage." I laughed. "I think they figured because I'm blind they didn't have to work so hard."

"You were fortunate in drawing the weakest player on the Grady team as your opponent in the finals," he stated. "Do you think you could have beaten either Wicks or Devereau if you'd drawn them?"

"I don't know. It's possible, but I'm glad I didn't have to test it. Jimmy Chang did a terrific job in beating Devereau. They're both great players. I'm just glad I didn't have to take my chances against either of them."

He asked a few more questions about how I play without being able to see the board and if I was planning to go into other tournaments. I fielded them as best I could, but I was glad when Jenny arrived with my pop and the reporter left.

"What did he want?" she asked when he was out of earshot.

"Just asking a bunch of questions about the tournament. I told him he should be talking to Jimmy; he's the star of the show."

"Wasn't he great?" she agreed and began replaying some of the exciting moves of the game.

A bunch of kids joined us, and for the next half hour I was the center of attention. Kids who had never spoken to me before came over and congratulated me. Even some of the people from my classes who had ignored me over the past few weeks made a point of being friendly to me. I felt great. Then, just to put the icing on the cake, I heard a chair being drawn up behind me and Hose's familiar voice in my ear.

"Congratulations, Hal. You were sensational."

"Hose! Where did you come from?" I exclaimed, turning around in my seat.

"I was at the next table. I didn't know if you'd want to talk to me, but I figured it wouldn't hurt to try."

"Not talk to you! Why wouldn't I want to talk to you?"

"Well, you've sure been avoiding me the past few weeks. Did I do something to make you mad, Hal?"

"No, of course not," I muttered. "I thought you were mad at me — you know, for not going to the dance with you."

"I was at first, but I figured you had your reasons. Anyway, I'm sure glad you're not mad. I really missed you. I was at the tournament both days and watched you win all your matches. I was so proud of you. Did you see the game last Saturday? Or do you watch basketball? I mean, do you listen to basketball? It must be pretty fast for you to follow, eh? Is baseball easier?" And he was off on a non-stop monologue. It was like music to my ears.

We arranged to get together the next day after school and I'd show him my computer chess game. Then another group of kids came over and he left.

I smelled her perfume before she spoke. "Hi, Hal." The husky voice and the velvet touch on my arm. "We're all so thrilled about the tournament, aren't we, Johnny?"

"Yeah. Nice going, Drucker. Now all you guys have to do is take the provincial."

"Oh, I'm sure they'll do that," Greer assured him. "With Hal on the team, they can't lose."

I said something modest and stupid, and a few minutes later they left. I sat there alone for about five minutes thinking of all the clever things I could have said and hadn't. Greer still had that ability to make me feel like a slow-witted gerbil whenever she was around. But she also reminded me of

Nancy and I suddenly felt a terrific sense of loss. It looked like the boycott of Hal Drucker was over, but would Nancy and I ever be close again?

When Keith and Jenny dropped me off a couple of hours later Mom met me at the door.

"Your father phoned from Vancouver, Hal," she said as she took my jacket and hung it in the hall closet. "He was very proud when I told him about your win. He was so sorry he couldn't have been there to see the match. I was too, dear." I didn't say anything as she led the way into the kitchen, where I could smell hot chocolate heating on the stove. "I hope you understand that we wouldn't have missed it if we could possibly have helped it. Your father's meeting was very important, and as I told you before, I couldn't leave until five. But that doesn't mean we weren't with you in spirit and pulling for you all the way."

"Sure, Mom," I said and dropped into the chair next to the table. The good feeling I had about the party began to fade and I started to get angry. "But Pete could have gone," I blurted out. I could hear the self-pity in my voice and hated it, but I couldn't seem to control myself. "He didn't even show up at the victory party. Practically all the Grade 11s were there, but my own brother couldn't be bothered."

"But Hal, he . . ."

"My recital was tonight, Hal, if you remember," Pete said softly from the doorway, cutting Mom off. "And I was at the tournament both days."

"You were?" I turned to him, baffled. "Why

didn't you say something? Let me know you were there?" I added, covering my embarrassment with anger.

"You haven't been exactly eager for my company, Hal. I figured you'd be happier if you didn't know I was around." He came over and sat down at the table. Mom went to the stove and poured the cocoa without comment, then left the room.

No one spoke as we sat across from each other sipping our cocoa. It was impossible for me to get any clue what Pete was thinking. That's one of the difficulties of being blind: there is no way you can read another person's body language. So much is said without words, and when you are unable to see you miss that silent communication. Finally, unable to stand the silence any longer, I spoke.

"I'm sorry, Pete. I guess I have been a little difficult the past couple of weeks."

"Yeah, you could say that," he answered tonelessly. No reassurance; no forgiveness; no explanation.

"But you've gotta admit I had good reason for being mad at you." My anger reared its head again at his lack of feeling.

"Oh? And what was that?"

"You have to ask?" The anger was now at full strength.

"If you're referring to the party, you're way out of line, Hal. Nobody did anything to put you on your high horse and send you scuttling to your room. You acted like a jerk."

"Oh, sure," I spat at him. "I suppose your little impromptu get-together had nothing to do with Mom and Dad's lecture about helping poor old Hal, the social outcast, have some fun. I wouldn't have minded if you had just had the party — in fact I would have been grateful to you for sharing your friends. But when I found out everyone knew what you were doing and why you were doing it, I was totally pissed with you."

Pete didn't answer for a moment. I heard him take another sip of cocoa and lean back on his chair. "Did you really believe I'd do a thing like that to you, Hal? God, what you must think of me!" He sighed. "Look, for your information, I didn't invite my friends over for your benefit, difficult as it may be for you to believe that. It's something I do every month or so. It had nothing to do with Mom and Dad."

He was either the greatest actor since Olivier or he was telling the truth. "Okay, so why didn't Nancy want me to know she was there? And what about that patronizing remark she made? It looks like the poor schmuck is having a good time. Don't tell me that wasn't a setup."

"Nancy didn't think you'd be very comfortable if you knew she was there, Hal. She thinks you resent her for some reason so she keeps out of your way. And," he added angrily, "she didn't call you a schmuck."

He had an answer for everything. And it all sounded so probable. Maybe Nancy did think I resented her. I hadn't been exactly charming the past few times we'd been together. And maybe Pete hadn't set up the party for me. I was beginning to get the first inkling that maybe I was a colossal egoist, thinking the whole world revolved around me.

"Okay, so I was out of line," I murmured. "But when I heard Mom and Dad coming on to you about helping me, I just naturally thought . . . Anyway, I guess I was wrong. I'm sorry."

"I'm sorry, too. I didn't know you'd heard that lecture the folks laid on me, Hal. It explains a lot." He got up and came around the table to put his hand on my shoulder. "And don't blame Nancy too much. She's a good kid."

You should know, I thought to myself with an unexpected twinge of jealousy. I knew I'd blown any chance I might have had, remote as it might have been, of dating her. She was Pete's girl now, and I might as well accept it.

"I don't blame her, Pete," I assured him. "I guess I've made a pretty big mess of things, haven't I?"

"Well, you didn't exactly get off to a roaring start," he agreed. "The way you took advantage of Hadley in the debate really turned a lot of people against you, you know. Then when all the teachers began treating you like you were something special and you acted like you agreed with them . . . well, I guess you get the point."

"But Gord . . ." I stopped. "Yeah, I get the point," I conceded as I remembered what Greer had said about putting someone down to look good.

"Anyway, that's water under the bridge now."

He gave my arm a punch. "The kids will have forgiven you everything for helping win the tournament. It's the first time Churchill has taken it in thirteen years. You're a real hero."

"No way," I disagreed. "The hero is Jimmy Chang. I had two easy matches and lucked out on the third. Jimmy had to beat Don Devereau for us to win, and he did."

"Maybe so, but you'll see. You won't have any more trouble with being snubbed again."

Boy, how wrong can a guy get!

Fifteen

There are two morning papers in our city. One, the *Gauntlet*, is pretty conservative, small c, and the other, the *Daily Courier*, is a lot like those tabloids you see in supermarket lineups. You know, full of pictures of half-naked women and articles on UFOs. Naturally my parents subscribe to the former.

When I came down for breakfast the next morning Dad was sitting at the table rustling the pages and muttering to himself. I was the last to arrive, since I'd slept in, having got home late from the party the night before. Pete was sitting in his usual seat and Mom was at the stove.

"Hurry up, Dad," Pete said as I came into the room. "I can't wait to hear what the paper says about the match."

"Just a minute — I'm trying to find it," Dad muttered. "Ah, here were are." I heard him fold the paper and shift in his chair. "'Churchill High takes Chess Tournament,'" he read.

"For the first time in thirteen years the team from Churchill High School won the inter-city chess tournament held this past weekend at the Convention Center. The crack team of Jimmy Chang, Jenny Gault, Keith Carradine and newcomer Hal Drucker overturned the formerly unbeatable Bishop Grady team in a playoff worthy of a grand championship. With the score even at the end of the first two playoff games in which Drucker overturned his opponent and Miss Gault was defeated, Churchill High's top player, Jimmy Chang, won his game in the tightest match of the tournament. The team will go on to play in the inter-provincial tournament in the fall. On a side note, Hal Drucker, who recently transferred to Churchill High and has been on the team for only a few weeks, is totally blind."

Dad put down the paper. "Well, what do you think of that?"

"Not a bad writeup," Pete answered, "but I don't think he gave enough credit to you, Hal. After all, you won all your games, too."

"I just wish they hadn't felt it was necessary to mention my blindness," I answered. "It makes me sound like a freak."

"Not at all, Hal," Dad disagreed. "It was only natural that they mention it. After all, it is quite an accomplishment, and they didn't make a big thing out of it."

"Yeah, I guess you're right." I was feeling so good about the way things were getting straightened out between me and Pete and Hose that nothing could bother me that morning. I was determined that when I got to school I was going to seek out Nancy and get that fixed up, too. I belted down my breakfast, managed not to spill or knock over a thing and was finished eating in about five minutes.

"Ready to go, Pete?" I asked as I was leaving the room.

The silence, as they say, was deafening. It was the first time I'd suggested that we walk to school together since the day of Pete's party.

"There's Nancy down at the end of the block," Pete informed me as we were walking down the front stairs. "Want to wait for her?"

I pretended not to hear as I made a big production out of getting my cane out of my book bag and opening it. Sure, I wanted to make up to Nancy for the way I'd been acting the past little while, but I wasn't convinced this was the time or place. Besides, it seemed that Nancy was Pete's girl now. I wasn't certain how I was going to handle that. The decision was taken out of my hands, however, when Nancy called out, "Hey, wait for me!"

I heard her running down the street toward us. We met on the sidewalk in front of the house.

"I read about the tournament, Hal," she announced, moving easily between Pete and me as we started down the street. "Congratulations. I was sorry I had to miss it, but I've been away all weekend. Just got home late last night. It must have been terribly exciting." She took my hand and squeezed it.

It was just as though the past weeks since that disastrous party at Greer's didn't exist. She was her friendly, warm self again, treating me the way she had when we first met. I was beginning to realize more and more what Pete meant by that remark about me not appreciating her. Okay, maybe she *was* Pete's girl now. I could still be friends with her. It would, I decided reluctantly, have to be enough.

She chatted on about the weekend she'd spent with her aunt and uncle on their farm, describing in wild detail the square dance she and her cousins had attended. By the time we arrived at school I was feeling so good that I was even ready to be friends with Gord Hadley.

By the time I got to homeroom I'd been congratulated by half a dozen kids and was grinning from ear to ear when I took my seat. Mr. McGregor came in a moment later and, after mentioning the tournament and making a reference to my part in it, got on with the business of taking attendance.

When he came to Hose's name I was surprised to discover he wasn't in class. I wondered if he was sick. He'd been fine the night before, but we had been late. He'd probably slept in, I decided.

If he had been in school that day, things sure would have turned out a lot differently.

* * *

I got the first inkling that something was wrong when I went into the science lab. When I got to the door I heard a group of kids talking near the door. The talking stopped as soon as I entered the room. No one spoke to me, which in itself was unusual. People had been coming up to me all morning to talk about the tournament. I shrugged and took my seat at my lab table. My lab partner, Jenny Gault, was already setting up the experiment we had been working on the previous week.

"Hi" I greeted her, expecting her usual cheery hello in return. She merely grunted and went on rattling test tubes. "Anything wrong?" I asked, wondering if I'd screwed up our experiment in some way and she'd just discovered it.

"Oh no, everything is just peachy," she answered in a tone that could have turned litmus paper red.

"What's the matter? Did I do something wrong?"

"You could say that." She paused, then, the irony gone from her voice, she continued, "I didn't think you were like that, Hal. Sure, I'd heard some of the kids talking about your rather inflated ego, but I figured it was just jealousy on their part. I guess I was wrong." She scratched a match and lit the Bunsen burner.

"But I don't understand."

"Forget it. I don't want to talk about it." She handed me a test tube and ordered me to fill it with liquid from the beaker in front of me. We didn't speak for the rest of the period except when it had to do with the experiment we were conducting.

It wasn't till I got to the lunch room that I found out what was going on.

I went directly to the table where Hose and I always sit, thinking he might just have been late getting to school that morning. But no one was at our table except a couple of giggling girls I didn't know. I hadn't brought my lunch, assuming that I'd be with Hose and he'd get it for me, so I was faced with attacking the lineup on my own. I waited for a while in case he'd been delayed. When it was pretty apparent he wasn't coming I decided I'd have to get my own food or starve. I got up and started toward the front of the room when someone took my arm and steered me back to the table.

"For gosh sake, Hal, why did you have to go and do such a dumb thing?" Pete's voice was half angry, half sad.

I sat down abruptly. This was getting ridiculous. First Jenny, then my own brother. "What the hell are you talking about? What am I supposed to have done?"

He sat down beside me and I heard him rustling a paper. "Listen to this," he ordered and began to read. "It's from the *Courier*."

"Churchill High School won its first chess tournament in over a dozen years yesterday afternoon. It was a stunning victory for the underdog Churchill team, beating the five-time winner Bishop Grady High. But to this reporter the real winner was seventeen-year-old Hal Drucker.

Hal, for those of you who don't know it, is totally blind. Yet this astonishing young man played three games of flawless chess, unable to see the board and with nothing to help him but his amazing memory.

"I spoke to young Drucker at the reception held last evening, and he told me he had learned to play chess from a kindly old teacher who had taken pity on him while he was attending the school for the blind where he was a student for ten years. I asked him how he felt about his opponents in the Saturday match and he had this to say: 'Ron Sykes was no problem. Boris Kamarov was a little more of a challenge, but I beat him easily.'

"'How about the finals?' I wanted to know. 'You had the weakest player. Do you think you could have won against either Wicks or Devereau?'

"'I don't think it would have been difficult,' he told me. 'In fact, I wish I'd had a chance to play a more challenging player. It would have been more fun.'

"Churchill High is fortunate to have acquired such an astonishing chess master for their sagging team. With Drucker aboard, who knows? They may take the inter-provincial title next fall."

He put the paper down and sighed.

"Pete," I cried, unable to believe what I'd just heard, "I didn't say those things! He completely misquoted me."

"Are you sure?" He sounded doubtful.

"Of course I'm sure. What kind of an egomaniac do you think I am, anyway?"

"But why would the guy deliberately twist your words?"

"I don't know! To sell papers, I suppose."

"Or maybe he didn't really twist your words at all." Nancy's voice came to me from across the table. "Honestly, Hal, I thought you were finally beginning to smarten up. Getting that old chip off your shoulder and not trying to make everyone look like a fool so you'd feel better about yourself. But I guess I was wrong." She started to walk away, then paused. "Coming, Pete? The drama club try-outs are on in about five minutes."

"Yeah, be right with you. Gee, Hal, why did you have to . . . ? Oh, never mind. See you at home tonight." And he left.

I was so angry that I could have bitten off the table leg. No wonder Jenny had been so cool. No wonder the congratulations had died off and the old shunning had started again. That dirty, lousy reporter, Parker something, taking everything I said and twisting it to make a good story. Not only did I come out looking like I had an ego the size of Toronto, but he made me sound pathetic, too, with his reference to the kindly old teacher who'd taken pity on me. It would have been funny if it hadn't been so awful. The "kindly old teacher" was a twenty-seven-year-old phys ed instructor with the personality of Attila the Hun.

I slumped back in my chair, my appetite gone,

and wondered what I was going to do. I didn't think I could stand to be treated like a leper again, especially after the way it had been after the tournament when people had been so friendly. I could have tried telling everyone that the story was a bunch of lies, but who'd buy that? Even my brother didn't believe me, so there wasn't much chance anyone else would, either. The old feeling of hopelessness crept over me, and I began thinking about quitting school and trying to get a job.

Then as I sat there the hopeless feeling gradually disappeared and was replaced with anger. Sure, I could leave and take a job, if I could get one. Let them win. But why should I give up my chance to make something of myself just because of what people thought of me? I didn't need them. I didn't need anybody — not Pete, not Nancy, not Hose, who must have read that stupid article and stayed home rather than face me.

I got up and left the cafeteria. No one was going to keep me from getting an education. I'd show them. I'd graduate at the top of my class and get into the best university in the country. I'd get a law degree and maybe someday be a judge. But right now I needed to get back at that sleazy reporter. I'd find him and make him wish he'd never heard of chess or me. I wasn't exactly sure what I would do: I only knew I needed to confront him face to face.

Sixteen

I left the cafeteria and found my way down to the office of the school secretary, the lady I'd almost knocked over the day Pete left me to go home alone. It seemed like another lifetime ago, so much had happened since.

"Yes, what can I do for you, young man?" she asked as I stood in the doorway waiting to be recognized.

"I was wondering if you could look up the address of the *Daily Courier* for me."

She didn't answer, but I heard her riffling through a book, which I assumed was the telephone directory.

"Ah, here it is!" she exclaimed a few moments later. "It's 10429 Oxford Street."

"Do you think you could call me a cab?"

"Oh, dear, that would be a very long and very expensive cab ride," she murmured. "The building is way over on the other side of town, right on the outskirts."

I reached in my pocket and brought out my wallet. I felt the bills and discovered I had a little less than ten dollars. Not nearly enough. "What bus would I take to get there?" I asked.

"Well, let's see now." More shuffling of papers. "According to the transit map, you'd take a downtown bus, then tranfer at Center and Sixth to a Bridgeport bus. It eventually turns onto 104 Avenue. Stay on till you reach Oxford Street, then get off and and walk a block north and you should be right in front of the building."

I thanked her and turned to go.

"Are you sure you can manage on your own, son?"

"Sure. No problem," I replied and hurried out the door.

Ten minutes later I was standing at the corner of Thirteenth and Grant waiting for the same bus that took Nancy and me to the mall.

I would have been pretty nervous under ordinary circumstances, but I was so angry and hurt that fear didn't have a chance of getting through. I asked the driver to let me off at the downtown transfer point and, after getting help from a woman waiting at the stop with me, hopped on the Bridgeport bus.

We went east for about half an hour and turned north. I was only half paying attention to the driver calling out the names of the streets as I mentally planned what I would say to Parker Cummings when I saw him. Then through the fog came "Next stop, Cambridge Street" and I got off. I pulled open my cane and started walking north. The end of the block dead-ended at a snow fence.

I was sure the secretary had said to walk one block north, but maybe it was one block east. I cursed myself for not paying more attention to her directions. I turned at the corner and started east.

A moment later I heard a car approaching from behind me and someone call out, "What do you think you're doing in the middle of the street — trying to get yourself killed?"

The sidewalk, such as it was, hadn't been shoveled and I'd obviously missed the curb and wandered into the street. Panicking, I turned and ran in the other direction, only to hit smack into the side of a building. The impact knocked me flat on my back in the snow, sending my cane flying out of my hand. I staggered to my feet, my head throbbing from the impact, and began groping around in the foot-high drifts, trying to find it. After ten minutes of fruitless searching I gave up.

I was soaked and half stunned from my fall; I began to shake, more from fear than cold, I guess. There had to be a door to the building, I reasoned, so I would feel my way along the side until I came to it. When I reached the corner I still hadn't found a door. Nothing but wooden siding, rough and splintery. I turned the corner and discovered my "building" was a high wooden fence. I crossed the side street, hoping to find a real building on the other corner, but there was nothing. I stood facing what I hoped was the street and waited for another car to pass. When I heard one coming I would move into the street and put up my hands. Surely someone would stop and help me.

I checked my watch; it was almost two-thirty. I stood there getting colder by the minute and wondering what I would do if no one came by. At three o'clock I gave up waiting and decided I would have to get moving or I'd freeze to death. I started walking.

The snow was getting deeper and harder to move through. My head was throbbing and I was dizzy. It was as quiet as a ghost town. There were no sounds of human habitation. No distant traffic noises, nothing. I might as well have been in the middle of the Arctic Circle. It finally filtered through my numb brain that I must have wandered into a field of some sort and was getting farther and farther away from civilization. I abruptly turned and started out in the opposite direction. Half an hour later I was still floundering around in foot-deep snow and totally disoriented.

By now I was chilled to the bone. A sharp wind had come up and had turned my light jacket and pants to ice. I could hear nothing to indicate I was still in the land of the living. What had happened? Where had I gone wrong? I got off the bus at Cambridge Street just as I'd been told. Or had I? Not that it made any difference now. I was apparently lost in some remote area of the city and no one even knew I was missing. It was ridiculous. I was in one of the largest cities in the country, and there was no one around to help me. The very real possibility that I could die of exposure flashed into my mind.

I stumbled on, getting more and more tired with every step, when my foot hit something solid. I reached down and felt what seemed to be a tree stump. Totally exhausted I sat down and buried my head in my hands. And for the first time since I was a child I cried.

When the tears finally dried up I tried to stand, but my body resisted. I collapsed back down onto the stump, the fear and the cold and the pain gradually taking over my whole body.

I was in a courtroom sitting on the judge's bench. I could see it all very clearly in my mind. Before me was Parker Cummings. He was on trial for libel and I was laughing crazily as I sentenced him to ten years writing obituaries in Alaska. Then the scene changed and I was sitting in the Convention Center auditorium at a chess board. Across from me was Nancy.

"It's your move," she said. I looked down at the board and saw that the chess pieces were ordinary enough except they all had heads of real people. I checked the position of the pieces and noticed that Nancy's King's Bishop was right in line with my Queen. I could take it easily. Then as I looked closer I saw her Bishop had Gord Hadley's head on it. I clutched my Queen and with a cry of triumph I started to move it.

"Don't!" Nancy yelled. "That's a terrible move."

I looked again and saw she was right. Taking her Bishop would lose me the game. But I would demolish Gord Hadley. I hesitated, holding the Queen in my hand and looking at Nancy. She said nothing but her eyes were pleading. I put the Queen down and as I picked up my knight I heard a faint cry off to my right.

"Hal! Is that you?"

I lifted my head and turned to the voice. It sounded like Nancy, but why was she so far away? And why had the Convention Center disappeared? My mind gradually began to clear and I heard it again.

"Stay right there, Hal. I'm coming." A moment later Nancy rushed up and grabbed my arm. "Oh, Hal, I've been so worried. Are you all right? You look frozen to death."

I staggered to my feet and fell against her. Nancy is six inches shorter and fifty pounds lighter than me, but somehow she managed to half carry, half drag me across the snow to her car.

"Quick, get in and put this blanket around you. The heater should warm you up soon." She opened the passenger door, and I collapsed onto the seat, feeling the blessed warmth envelop me.

"Here's your cane," she said laying it beside me as she climbed into the driver's seat. "I found it on the sidewalk. That's how I figured out it was you wandering around halfway up the hill behind the deserted stockyards. What were you doing up there, anyway?"

I tried to speak but my teeth were chattering so

hard that I couldn't form words. Nancy drove in silence, waiting for me to thaw out.

"How did you know where I'd gone?" I was finally able to croak.

"Easy," she replied. "When someone told me you weren't in class this afternoon I figured you'd just gone home. I wouldn't have blamed you after the way everyone treated you. Anyway, I went to the office to see if you'd booked off sick and Miss Andress, the secretary, told me you'd been asking about the *Courier* offices. So I put two and two together."

"Okay, but what are you doing out here?"

She didn't say anything for a moment, then I heard her sigh.

"I phoned the *Courier* office to try to catch you before you left. I figured you could use a ride home. When they told me you hadn't shown up, I got worried, so I came looking for you."

"The Lone Ranger to the rescue, eh?" I asked, unable to keep the bitterness out of my voice. "Poor old Hal — leave him on his own for a minute and he's lost."

Nancy apparently chose to ignore my self-pitying remark. "You haven't answered my question. What were you doing in that field. You're four blocks from the *Courier* building."

"I don't know what went wrong. I got off at Cambridge Street just like the secretary told me. She must have made a mistake."

"The *Courier* building is on Oxford Street, Hal. It wasn't her mistake; it was yours."

I started to protest, then realized she was probably right. I'd screwed up again all by myself. I couldn't do anything right.

Too exhaused to talk any more, I laid my head on the seat back and fell asleep.

Seventeen

*I*t wasn't until much later that evening that I became aware of my surroundings. I had apparently passed out in the car and didn't remember anything after Nancy had told me I'd got off at the wrong stop. I vaguely remembered the doctor coming to see me and Mom and Dad standing around my bed looking stricken. I tried to reassure them I was okay, but my voice didn't seem to be working.

Now I was lying in my bed eating a bowl of soup, surrounded by my whole family. My foot had a touch of frostbite and I was suffering from shock. I knew they were all wanting to know what had happened to me, but I just wasn't up to talking yet. At least not to explaining how I had screwed up yet again. As they stood there looking anxious and more than a little curious I sipped my soup and said nothing. Finally the silence seemed to get to them. Dad spoke.

"When I got home a little after five and found no one here I was a bit surprised," Dad began to explain. "But I just assumed you and Pete had gone off somewhere and would be home any minute. When you hadn't come home by five-thirty I phoned your mother, thinking you might have told her where you were going."

"I came home immediately," Mom interjected, picking up the story. "I found Pete's note saying that the band was going to rehearse right through dinner and not to expect him home until eight. Naturally I began to panic. I was just about to call the police when Nancy rang the doorbell and told us you had passed out in the front seat of her car. We managed to get you in and up to bed, then we called the doctor. You were so white and your breathing was hoarse and shallow. I was so afraid you were going to . . ." She began to cry.

"It's all right now, dear," Dad murmured, patting her clumsily on the shoulder. "He's home and he's going to be fine. We're very anxious to know what happened, Hal. Nancy told us where she'd found you, but we can't understand what you were doing way over on the far side of town. She said you would tell us when you recovered.

I knew they were all dying to know. "I guess you're wondering what happened." (The under-statement of the year.) "See, I was trying to get to the *Courier* office," I began, taking the last spoon-ful of soup and putting the bowl on the tray in front of me. "I guess I got off at the wrong stop. I didn't realize what had happened until I tried to find the building and it wasn't where it was supposed to be." I paused, waiting for a response. None came, so I continued, relating everything that had happened from hitting the fence to giving up and sitting down on the tree stump in the field. Telling it, I knew, was the best way to free myself from the horror of it.

When I finally finished, Mom put her hand on my forehead and smoothed back my hair. "You poor darling." Her voice was choked with tears. "When I think what could have happened to you I—"

"But nothing did, thank God," Dad interrupted. "What I don't understand, however, is why you were going to the *Courier* office in the middle of the day?"

"I think I know the answer to that," Pete said. "It was because of the newspaper article, wasn't it?"

"Yeah, that and a lot of other stuff." The memory of that morning came rushing back: Jenny's words in the science lab; Nancy's anger; Pete's disgust. And all over something that wasn't my fault. I'd had a nightmare experience that afternoon, but it hadn't changed my resolve to keep my distance from my schoolmates and concentrate entirely on graduating at the top of my class. No more chess; no more stupid parties. I'd be a loner, and to hell with everyone. I leaned back on the pillows and closed my eyes. At that moment the doorbell rang and a few minutes later Nancy came into the room.

"Hi," she said, sounding more cheerful than she had for weeks. "How are you feeling?"

"Not bad," I answered a bit uncertainly. "I guess I owe you a big thank-you for rescuing me. Thanks, Nancy," I muttered, feeling stupid and uncomfortable.

"All in a day's work," she answered airily, and I heard her pull a chair up to the end of the bed.

"And I owe you a gigantic apology," Pete said. "I should have known you wouldn't sound off the way the article said you did."

"What are you talking about, Peter?" Dad's voice was tinged with anger.

"The article in the *Courier*. I guess you guys didn't see it. It was totally misleading and made Hal look like a real jerk. Some of the kids saw it and the word got around." He paused and I heard him squirm in his chair. "Even I thought it was true."

"And you don't now?" I asked, puzzled.

"No, and neither does anyone else at school. Hose set us all straight."

"Hose? But he was away today."

"Only in the morning. He slept in and his mom let him take the morning off, but he showed up for afternoon classes. I guess it didn't take long for word of the article to get to him and when he read it for himself he went berserk."

"He came storming into math class waving the paper in the air and yelling at the top of his voice." Nancy took up the story. "Mr. Babcock made him calm down and explain what was causing him to hyperventilate all over the room. That's when he told us about overhearing that guy Parker Cummings interviewing you at the party. He said the dweeb had taken everything you said and twisted it to make a good story. He told us that you'd given all the credit for the victory to Jimmy, for one thing. And that business about you saying your competition was a pushover was a complete lie. By the time school was over for the day everyone at Churchill High had heard about it. I can't tell you how sorry I am for what I said at lunch. I hope you'll forgive me."

"Me too, Hal." Pete's voice was barely audible. "If only I hadn't been such a schmuck and had trusted you."

"Are you telling me that you're responsible for Hal's running off yesterday and nearly getting himself killed?" Dad's anger was at full power now. "My God, Peter. How much more damage are you going to do to Hal before you learn some responsibility?"

"I'm sorry." The guilt that I so hated filled his voice. Suddenly I couldn't stand it any longer.

"Why the hell should you feel sorry?" I demanded, my voice rising to a fever pitch. "Nothing is your fault. It was only natural that you should believe what the paper said, but you weren't the only reason I ran off." I paused and took a deep breath. "I'm so damned sick of you taking guff from Mom and Dad for everything that happens to me. Why don't you ever stand up for yourself? Don't you see how much I hate it when you knuckle under? It makes me feel even more of a cripple. Why do you *do* it?"

There was total silence for about ten seconds.

Then Pete's voice, soft and full of emotion whispered, "How can you ask that, Hal, when you know I'm the one who caused your blindness?"

Eighteen

"What are you *talking* about?" I yelled, sitting up in bed and knocking my tray on the floor. "Have you gone crazy?"

"Oh, Hal, don't pretend it's not true."

"Of course it's not true. Pete, you weren't even around when I had that accident with the firecrackers."

"Damn right I was! I remember it like it was yesterday. I waved a firecracker in your face and it blinded you."

"Pete!" Mom cried out. "Where did you ever get that idea? You didn't *have* any firecrackers. You were only allowed sparklers."

"Sure," I said, nodding in agreement. "You were bugging me with that stupid sparkler — pushing it into my face and waving it around until I told you to get lost. It was just after that that I lit the match and the whole bunch of firecrackers blew up in my face."

"That's right, Pete." Dad's voice had lost all its anger and he sounded confused. "Mrs. Macphee from across the street saw the whole thing. It was she who rushed over and brought Hal into the house."

"But I remember it so well — everyone telling me to stop making trouble. You and Mom not talking to me. Sending me off to Grandma Perkins."

"Oh, Pete, honey." Mom started to cry and I heard her walk over to the chair where my brother was sitting. "We were all so upset about Hal that we weren't paying much attention to you, I guess. We sent you to Gran's so we could be at the hospital with Hal. Oh, Lord!" she murmured. "Have you been thinking all these years that you . . ."

"What else could I think?" Pete asked. "You've always told me I owed it to Hal to help him, take care of him, give him anything he wanted."

"But son, we never meant it like that." Dad was sounding as distressed as Mom. "We only meant you should watch out for your brother. Help him if he needed help."

"So that's why you never complained when Mom or Dad asked you to do anything for me?" I muttered half to myself. "Why you never seemed to mind when I got things and you didn't?"

"Not exactly, Hal. I didn't mind that the folks bought you stuff. After all, its been a lot easier for me. I didn't get sent halfway across the country to live in a school for the blind. I can read and play sports and do anything I want to do."

"So can Hal." Nancy's voice broke in quietly. No

one spoke. I guess we'd forgotten she was in the room, what with Pete's incredible revelation.

"That's a stupid thing to say, Nancy," I said, breaking the silence and miffed that she should be bringing up the whole "Hal is perfectly normal" crap at a time like this. Mom and Dad obviously agreed with me.

"I'm sure you mean well, dear," Mom soothed, "but I don't think you quite understand the situation."

"Maybe I don't, but I do know that Hal has been hiding behind his handicap for too long. If he doesn't stop using it as an excuse to get out of facing and overcoming his problems he'll end up with a far greater disability than blindness."

"Young lady, I think perhaps you'd better leave now," Dad announced. "We very much appreciate what you did to find Hal, but we're in the middle of a family discussion that really doesn't concern you."

"No," I said. "Let her explain. What do you mean I've been hiding behind my handicap? What do you expect me to do? Go out for the football team? Or maybe join the drama club?"

"Not a bad idea — the second option, I mean. If you don't want to be an actor — although there's no reason why you couldn't; other blind people have — you could work behind the scenes. The point is there are a million ways you could become involved in the school, in the community, but instead you refuse to take a chance."

"Young lady!" Dad was angry. "I'll thank you —

"Wait a minute," I interrupted. "What about the chess club? I joined it, didn't I?"

"That doesn't count. It wasn't a challenge. You didn't have to put yourself on the line — take a chance of ending up looking stupid or embarrassed."

"Oh, you mean like at Greer's party," I scoffed.

"Exactly. You acted like a jerk. Not because you spilled your drink," she added as I started to interrupt, "but because you ran away. You're always running away without bothering to find out what's really going on." She pushed her chair back and walked over to the door. "I'm sorry if I sounded off, but I'm so darned tired of watching you isolate yourself from everyone and everything because of your stupid pride."

"It's not pride!" I shouted. "I do what I want to do and I do it without any help. I don't need you or anyone else. Can't you understand that?"

"No, I can't. Everyone needs help at one time or another and you need a special kind of help. There's nothing shameful about that."

"I repeat," I answered, gritting my teeth," I don't need anyone."

"Okay, if you say so, Hal, but did it ever occur to you that maybe we need you?"

Before I could form an answer, the door shut behind her.

"Well, I declare!" Mom exclaimed, sounding for all the world like Grandma Perkins. "What an extraordinary child!"

"She had no right to talk to you like that, Hal,"

Dad put in. "Especially after all you've been through. You'd think she'd have more consideration. She was totally out of line. Talking through her hat."

"No, you're wrong, Dad," Pete disagreed. "Everything Nancy said was right on. Hal does hide behind his handicap and you encourage it."

"Now you just hold on a minute, Peter. That's a pretty serious accusation you're making. Your mother and I want only what's best for Hal."

"I know that, but what you think is best may not *be* best. Remember when Hal first came home and you wanted me to be in all his classes? That's the kind of thing I mean, where you're taking his independence away from him."

"But we thought it would be easier for him if you —

"Hold it," I interrupted. "This is getting too heavy and I'm tired. Could we postpone the in-depth analysis of the Halford Drucker predicament until later." I lay back on my bed and turned away from them.

"Certainly, dear," Mom murmured solicitously. A moment later I heard the door open and close behind them.

I lay there thinking about what Nancy had said and having a conversation with my alter ego until Mom came up with a cup of warm milk a couple of hours later.

Weren't you really using your handicap to avoid facing the real world? my alter ego demanded. Wasn't your fear of failure, of humiliation, keeping you from involving yourself with people? Taking chances, as Nancy put it?

Maybe so, but when I did take chances, look what happened; I got myself lost and had to be rescued.

Sure you did, but what about swallowing your pride and asking someone to go with you instead of storming off by yourself? It was a stupid, thoughtless thing to do.

Okay, so maybe I need to ask for help a little more. But what about getting involved with the school? She was really off base on that one. What can a blind guy contribute?

Uh-oh. Here comes that self-pity again. You know you have a lot of talent in many areas that you haven't tried to capitalize on. Remember at the school for the blind when you wrote, directed and starred in that one-act play? Everyone said you were great.

Yeah, but that was at the school. I only looked good because everyone else looked so bad. I'd make a fool of myself if I tried anything like that at Churchill High.

Make a fool of yourself? That's what it's all about, isn't it? You're scared to death of doing anything that will make you an object of pity or of ridicule. But everyone is in that position one time or another. Remember Nancy's story about her grandfather and the fur coat? He couldn't have looked sillier, but apparently he passed the whole thing off as a joke. He laughed at himself and so everyone else laughed with him, not at him.

Okay, so maybe you've got a point. Now, what do I do about it?

You know what you have to do. Get involved. Put yourself on the line. Start by apologizing to Nancy for the way you've treated her. You might even apologize to Gord Hadley for taking advantage of him at the debate.

Oh, no. That's asking too much. The Gord Hadley thing, I mean. But I guess I should apologize to Nancy. She's a good friend. I kinda wish she could be more, but she's Pete's girl now. Besides, why would any girl want to get involved with a blind guy?

There you go again. Do you imagine every blind person in the country is single and celibate?

No, I guess not, but —

No more buts. You've hidden behind buts and howevers and if-onlys for long enough. It's time to start acting like a man instead of a scared little kid who can't function without his teddy bear. And for once admit that you do need people.

Mom came in about that time and saved me from having to face and accept that one. As I drank the milk I began dismissing all the arguments why I should change, why I should force myself to make an effort. There was no reason that I shouldn't carry on as I'd planned on my own. I'd study hard, graduate at the top of my class, forget all about the social scene. Why should I put myself in a position of getting hurt? Pretty soon I was right back where I started before I had that conversation with myself.

You can forget all that stupid talk about getting

involved because it's good for you, I told my alter ego. I don't need anybody.

Then after I'd finished the milk and started to fall asleep my alter ego had the final say. Over and over it whispered Nancy's words in my head. "Did it ever occur to you that maybe *we* need *you*?"

Nineteen

T he next day I waited out in front of the house
till Nancy came along and we walked to
school together. At first it was a little
strained. Both of us had said a lot of things we were
sorry for. I wanted to tell her I knew she was right
about me needing to get involved, take a chance,
and most of all, not be afraid to ask. But it was still
pretty tough for me to admit that maybe I was
wrong. She wasn't making it any easier, either. We
walked for a couple of blocks without exchanging
a word. Finally I broke the ice.

"About that club you belong to: PURE, HARM-
LESS, whatever you call it . . ."

"SAFE," she answered with a smile in her voice.
"Students Advocating a Fit Environment. Why?"

"Well, I was wondering if you still need somebody to help with the slogans and stuff."

She didn't say anything for about half a block.
Then she put her arm through mine and answered,

"Yeah, we sure do. Did you have someone in mind?"

I knew then I didn't have to apologize to her about anything. She'd already forgiven me for all the stupid things I'd done.

It felt so good walking along with her like that. She continued talking about the club and what it was doing, and I used the excuse that I couldn't hear her very well, what with the traffic noises, to bend down close to her. Her hair smelled like fresh strawberries and when I casually brushed my face against it, it was as soft and silky as rose petals.

I was half in a daze, paying little attention to what she was saying and wondering why I'd never noticed how low and husky her voice was when I heard Pete calling for us to wait up. Then reality struck. Nancy was Pete's girl. She was only being kind. I had no right to assume she had any interest in me other than as her boyfriend's brother. I pulled my arm away and opened my cane.

"Hey, Hal!" Pete exclaimed as he rushed up to join us. "How come you took off without waiting for me?" Then he stopped and I heard his low chuckle. "Well, excuse me. I didn't mean to interrupt."

I expected Nancy to assure him he wasn't interrupting anything, but she was silent.

"Well, carry on," Pete continued, and the low chuckle turned into a laugh. "See you later." And he was gone.

I didn't understand, and I guess it must have shown on my face. Nancy took my hand. "Don't back away again, Hal. It's okay."

"But what about you and Pete? I thought you were . . ."

"Pete's a good friend, that's all. It's you I've . . ." She paused and removed her hand from mine. "Oh, what's the use. You can't see anyone but Greer Jordan."

I had a momentary urge to snap back, I can't see her, either. Then the meaning of that half-finished sentence hit me. She was more than just interested in me as Pete's brother: poor blind Hal. And she was just as unsure of herself as I was: poor scared Nancy. I began thinking of all the people I'd met since I came home to stay. None of them had a physical disability like me, but I finally under-stood — they all had their own emotional disabil-ity: poor guilty Pete; poor shy Hose; even poor dumb Gord Hadley. I wasn't really unique at all. Sure, I had difficulty with things other people took for granted, but that didn't make me any less a person.

I was as good as anyone, even Johnny Sterling, and I could have anyone I wanted, even Greer Jordan.

But, I thought with a grin, I didn't want Greer Jordan.

I reached over and took Nancy's hand and tucked it into my arm.

"Now about the spring dance," I began. "It's coming up in a few weeks. Will you go with me?"

Nancy squeezed my arm and laughed.

"Why, Hal, I thought you'd never ask!"